The rain came down so hard that Slocum could scarcely see ten feet ahead. When they were almost to the top of the hill, he heard Velarde say, "I don't think those are trees, señor."

"What the hell else would they be?"

Lightning flamed, searing the prairie nearby. "¡Madre de Dios!" Velarde whispered, and somehow Slocum heard him clearly.

They were not trees. Not natural ones, at least. Three tau crosses stood at the crown of the hill. From each was suspended the naked body of a man.

OTHER BOOKS BY JAKE LOGAN

JAKE LOGAN

SLOCUM'S DRIVE

BERKLEY BOOKS, NEW YORK

DEDICATION

*For Joseph,
foremost parishioner
of the Reverend Hezekiah*

SLOCUM'S DRIVE

A Berkley Book/published by arrangement with
the author

PRINTING HISTORY
Berkley edition/February 1983

ISBN: 0-425-05998-7

A BERKLEY BOOK® TM 757,375
The name "BERKLEY" and the stylized "B"
with design are trademarks belonging to
Berkley Publishing Corporation.

PRINTED IN THE UNITED STATES OF AMERICA

1

A rifle boomed from the cutbank of the nameless stream. Four hundred yards ahead of the herd the lead rider slumped from his saddle as bonelessly as a sack of meal.

As John Slocum yanked his Henry rifle from its scabbard he heard the foremost longhorns start to raise a panicky lowing at the shot and the smell of blood. "Stay close to them steers," he shouted back over his shoulder at his drovers. "Don't let 'em stampede!"

Without waiting for acknowledgment he dug his big Mexican rowels into his pony's flanks. The scrubby little paint dropped his haunches and lit out across the prairie like a jackrabbit, heading straight for the wash that lay like a knife slash across the path of the great herd. *They say a Texas wrangler'll die for his herd*, he thought. *Hope that ain't bushwah*. He jacked a round into the rifle's chamber.

He'd been on either side of ambushes enough that this one didn't worry him. Some bravo with buck fever had blown off a round much too early, alerting the intended victims to the waiting trap. It had been tough for Jimmie Fitzhugh, lying up there in the bluestem by the stream with his blood soaking into the clay. From here on it was going to be a whole lot tougher for the man or men who'd gunned him down like a dog.

If Slocum's men didn't lose control of the herd, that was. Weighing in at near a thousand pounds apiece, with horns as long as a tall man's arms outspread, the two thousand five hundred head of J-Bar-C steers Slocum and his crew were driving to the Abilene railhead would leave the cowhands as so many greasy smears on the prairie if they spooked and stampeded.

Flame, blossoming like an exotic flower, sprouted from the near stream bank. The shot went wide of Slocum. Bending low over his saddle horn, he galloped on. As he passed the chuck wagon, midway between the herd and the stream, he heard the boom of Cookie Cantwell's huge Sharps single-shot pistol and the protesting squeals of the mules over whose heads the cook had fired. The big, hang-bellied cook was standing in the driver's box stuffing another cartridge into the breech as Slocum flashed past.

Slocum chanced a glance over his shoulder. Neither anger at the shooting of Fitzhugh nor a sense of self-preservation had made the handpicked wranglers abandon their charges. As if on command, a pair of riders were racing to his aid while the rest circled the drove, singing wordlessly to calm the skittish beasts. He grinned in satisfaction. If love of duty or love of life weren't enough, the promise of a share in the hundred dollars of good yellow gold that rested on each and every six-foot rack of horns was more than ample to keep the men at their posts.

Motion to his left caught his eye as he turned his face forward again. His grin turned to a snarl. The horses of the remount herd, which had been paralleling the drove and staying roughly even with the chuck wagon, were streaming off into the west along the stream, chivvied by a colorfully dressed drover. *No-good Mexican son-*

ofabitch! thought Slocum in a blaze of anger. *He's runnin' away!*

But there was no time for the coward now. Now was the time for action.

Two shots went off practically in his face. He felt the hot breath of a bullet's passage. Dallying his reins twice around the saddle horn, Slocum shouldered the Henry and opened up, firing as fast as he could work the lever. A lanky, towheaded man stood up suddenly behind the bank, threw his hands into the air, and fell back with a squelch in the mud.

With cries of dismay the dead man's companions broke and ran. Slocum sawed hard on the reins, bringing his paint to a rearing halt on the verge of the clay bank. At the water's edge one of the running figures halted and spun round, leveling a Spencer carbine from the hip. Slocum had an impression of white-blond hair, a tear-streaked young face contorted into a mask of hatred. *It's just a kid*, flashed through his mind.

But a colt can kill you just as dead as a full-grown stud. The Henry cracked once. The right side of the boy's flannel shirt exploded in red, and he dropped to lie with the sun-warmed water lapping gently at his chest and stirring his pale hair.

The third bushwhacker, a dark-haired man with a roll of fat jiggling like pudding above his suspendered pants, had thrown away his weapon and slogged into the middle of the slow-rolling stream, leaving a trail of tan silt stirred up in his wake. There was clearly no more fight left in him than there was wine in a broken bottle. Slocum decided the hell with him and started to swing down off his horse.

A pistol boomed behind John Slocum. The running

man grunted and went face-first into the water. A red cloud swirled up around the humped island of his rump, mingling with the earth-brown water and the lighter silt. Slocum's boot heel thumped the dirt, and he turned, feeling the muscles of his cheeks go taut.

A few yards behind him Cord Blaylock sat his horse, showing teeth through his prematurely gray-flecked brown mustache in a look of satisfaction. His white-stockinged black stallion tossed its head and pranced nervously at the smell of the blue smoke curling out of the muzzle of his Shawk & McLanahan .44.

"That's one yellow-bellied sodbuster won't go bush-whackin' no more droves," he announced in a Tennessee twang.

For a moment Slocum locked Blaylock's hazel eyes with his own gunmetal-gray ones. Then he let go the reins and walked to where the wounded drover lay facedown in the grass by the cutbank. From ten feet he could see that Fitzhugh's chest wasn't stirring with the up-and-down motion of breathing. He knelt by his side and rolled him over gently with his free hand. The young man's eyes were closed. His mouth gaped life-lessly. He was only nineteen, and with his face relaxed by death looked younger still. Slocum straightened slowly, lightly gripping the Henry with both hands. Fitz-hugh had been a fair-haired boy on his first overland drive, always laughing and full of fun, but a steady hand, reliable under pressure when the sky was black and the lightning clawed the prairie and the steers bawled and rolled their eyes in a frenzy of fear so thick it clogged a man's throat like dust to be around it. Tra-ditionally, a green kid like Fitzhugh would have spent the drive riding drag, eating dust at the rear of the herd all the way to Abilene. Slocum was trail boss for this drive, and Slocum didn't give two hoots in hell for tradition; he rotated his men from position to position, so that each one had experience as everything but cook.

Of course, if Jimmie Fitzhugh hadn't been doing his first brief stint as lead rider today he'd still be alive. But Slocum and every man on the drive had signed on knowing that this run would be dangerous, more dangerous than any drive they'd ever been on. And he'd seen too many young men die for this death to affect him much.

He heard his name called and looked off up the stream. Two riders were approaching along the muddy flat verge. He frowned. The one on the left—a slender rider sitting tall on a chestnut stallion, with a Winchester held in one hand and black hair that was long even by the standards of a Texas cowboy spilling down from beneath the flat brim of a black Andalusian hat—he had seen racing up behind him when he charged the bushwhackers. That was bad enough, but the rider to the right—

"Velarde!" He spat the name out like a piece of rotten meat. "What brings you crawling back? The way you lit out, I thought you'd be halfway to Guadalajara by now."

He watched the other intently, half hoping that his bitter words would be taken as a challenge. He'd never liked the Mexican with his gaudy scarf, fancy leather pants, and boots tooled in intricate patterns of eagles and crosses. Now he was mad enough to kill him on the spot.

But Velarde's delicate-looking brown right hand stayed where it was, resting easily on his hip, and made no move toward the worn ivory grip of the Dragoon hanging a few inches away. His lean face split in a smile. His teeth were startlingly bright against the darkness of his face.

"It pleases Señor Slocum to make a joke," he said.
Slocum stiffened. The Mexican gunslinger never spoke
in that stilted formal way unless he was mocking someone. "I was driving the *remuda* out of the way, so that
they wouldn't spook and bolt into the herd. That would
start a stampede *muy pronto*—but of course you know
that, señor."

Slocum's face turned hotter than the August sun.
Velarde had saved the drove from disaster—and the
thought had never crossed Slocum's mind. A real
cowhand would have known at once what the Mexican
was doing. But Slocum was no cowboy, and everybody
knew it.

The crying of the steers was growing quieter as the
herd settled down. Raging at himself for revealing his
ignorance, Slocum swung toward the other rider, who
was getting off the chestnut. "What in God's name do
you think you're doing, charging up into the fight like
that? You might've got killed."

The black-haired rider gave him a cool green gaze. "I
was trying to turn their flank. That was the right thing
to do, wasn't it?"

"Don't change the subject. Why'd you take the
risk?"

The rider removed the hat, shook back glossy hair,
and laughed. It was a clear, lovely, feminine laugh. It
went quite well with the long-legged high-breasted
feminine body, the finely sculptured face. It didn't go
well worth a damn with the rigors and dangers of a
cattle drive. Especially *this* drive.

"I didn't come on this drive to be safe, Mr. Slocum,"
the young woman said. "I came along to help ensure
that my father's herd reached the railhead in Abilene in
time to earn the Frenchman's bonus." She paused.
"The same reason as you."

He looked at her for a moment, then turned away. "No," he said roughly. "I came for the money."

She said nothing. With a thumping of unshod hooves, a heavy jangle of harness, and the groaning squeak of brake on axle, Cookie Cantwell brought the chuck wagon to a halt a few yards from the lip of the cutbank. His little colorless eyes scanned the far bank for further signs of danger. One black-furred paw engulfed the butt of his Sharps.

"They all gone?" he asked. Slocum nodded. "How's Jimmie?"

"Dead."

The burly cook clucked mournfully. "Thass a shame. How 'bout them damned sodbusters—beggin' your pardon, Miss Callahan."

"Two of 'em are done for, I think." As the herd had come back under control, several more drovers had ridden up to see what was going on. Slocum told them to see to burying Jimmie.

The black-haired woman had shoved her Winchester 66 back in its cordovan scabbard and scrambled down the bank to kneel by the wounded boy's side. He shook his head and moaned as she examined him with deft, gentle fingers. "He's badly hurt," she said.

Slocum rubbed his jaw. "Put him in the wagon and tend to him."

"Put him in the wagon!" Blaylock's voice rang with incredulity like a silver dollar dropped on a polished mahogany bar. "But the little varmint killed Jimmie!"

Slocum gazed at him without expression. "Put him in the wagon," he repeated levelly.

As a couple of wranglers dismounted to help the woman, Slocum said, "We've had it easy too long. Now's the hard part. Here's where we start earning our pay, boys. It's three hundred miles to Abilene—three hundred miles of rustlers, jayhawkers, and sodbusters who see Texas fever in every steer from south of Indian Territory. We better look sharp from here on in—or we could all wind up like Jimmie Fitzhugh."

Digging the trench for Jimmie's grave or just lounging around waiting for Cookie to break out the hardtack and cold beans for lunch, the men looked at Slocum and then at each other. His words struck through them like cold steel. An icy wind seemed to blow from the yawning grave.

Santiago Velarde dropped nimbly from his high-cantled Mexican saddle and knelt to scoop up a handful of yellow dirt. He held it up for all to see. "Welcome to Kansas, señores," he said, and laughed.

2

"But I'm not a wrangler," John Slocum had protested on that cool indigo evening two weeks before. A clean, piny breeze blew in through open windows, carrying the soft lowing of cattle and the cries of the first nightbirds as they wheeled and dipped to catch the mosquitoes rising from the brook that ran past the adobe ranchhouse. The last beaten-copper cutting of the sun had disappeared behind the Sangre de Cristos, and the valley was at peace.

A Mexican woman moved through the *sala*, silent as the breeze, lighting the kerosene lamps one by one. Polished silver reflectors threw a yellow glow and brought the heavy-beamed ceiling to life with shadows. Joe Callahan ran a hand that might have been carved from a block of granite through his grizzled close-cut red hair, and laughed.

"No, but you're the man for the job," he said. "Will you hear me out?"

Slocum looked from the man in the wheeled chair to the tall, slender woman who stood beside Callahan's blocky right shoulder. Grudgingly he nodded and sat in a hefty carved-oak chair covered with a gray-and-black patterned Indian blanket. Even if Joe Callahan hadn't been a friend of some years' standing, he was Kevin

Callahan's father, and that was enough to entitle any man to John Slocum's hearing.

"I doubt if you pay much attention to European politics." Slocum acknowledged the fact with a brief grin, and accepted a huge tumbler of whiskey from the gaunt serving woman, who clutched her black mantilla about her shoulders as if the evening cool chilled her to the bone. "Well, for some time now the French and the Prussians have been snarling at each other across their borders like two mongrels over a bitch in heat. Two days ago they went for each other's throats. France declared war and Prussia invaded. The smart boys with the eastern papers all say that Napoleon III will make short work of the Germans, but I have my doubts."

He paused to take a glass of whiskey for himself. With a pair of tongs he took several chunks of ice from the icehouse out back out of a pewter bucket, with a boyish grin of apology at this sign of weakness. Slocum said nothing. Joe Callahan had fought in the Mexican War and gone on to carve the J-Bar-C out of the highlands of the Raton Plateau in eastern Mora County, New Mexico Territory, against the best efforts of Kiowa, Comanche, and Jicarilla Apache. Principle had kept him out of the War of Secession, just as it had sent his only son off to die before Cemetery Ridge on a hot June day in 1863. His iron will and that alone had kept him firmly in charge of the sprawling ranch after his horse threw him and broke his back after being spooked by a rattler in '65. For twenty-one years a fiery Louisiana beauty named Desirée LaSalle had been his wife and never strayed an inch from his side; since the fever had taken her the same year the war swallowed up their son, he had been raising their daughter Elianora on his own as best he could, and the proud carriage and challenging eyes of the beautiful young woman standing by his side showed that he had done that job well too. Joe Callahan was a *man*, a strong man, and as far as John Slocum was concerned he had no need to apologize to anybody.

"Yesterday I received a telegram. An agent of the French government, a Colonel LeBlanc, will be arriving in Abilene in a month to buy beeves for the French army. The Frenchies got caught with their britches down—they're desperate for supplies. The price he'll be paying is one hundred dollars a head. In gold."

A long, low whistle escaped Slocum's lips. He was a tall, rangy, rawboned proposition who looked at the world with eyes the color of a Bowie knife blade and the cynical reserve of one whose youth was early burned away in the fires of battle. He had a long, weathered face whose high cheekbones hinted at a touch of Indian blood, as did its apparent agelessness: He could have been anywhere from twenty-five to fifty, though in fact he was twenty-nine. It was a face that didn't give much away. Now it gave Callahan a look of sheer awe. *One hundred dollars.* That was three times the best premium prices paid at any Kansas railhead—and in gold, at a time when paper money was starting to lose value as soon as it came off the presses.

"Won't that bring the droves in like flies to a horse carcass?" Slocum asked skeptically.

Callahan shook his big head. "Most of the ranches that were going to drive have already done so. And no more are likely to, with the new Texas fever scare on. The sodbusters are up in arms, even in the zone the Kansas legislature approved for driving Texas herds through, and rumor says the jayhawkers are out again. I heard that half the drovers went out with the big drives in '66 never came back. Least that's what happened to my boys. Word is that any drives trying to reach Abilene now will make the ones that year look like a Sunday drive to church.''

"What about the animals they got in feedlots up in Kansas?'' Slocum asked.

This time it was the raven-haired Elianora who spoke. "Those steers are all contracted for,'' she said in that low, husky voice. It ran down Slocum's spine like fingers. He looked away from her clear green eyes and took a hurried gulp of whiskey. "The Chicago slaughterhouses won't take kindly to any breaches of those contracts, and neither would a jury. Especially on behalf of the French. The trouble in Mexico wasn't that long ago.''

A muscle ticked in Slocum's jaw and he nodded.

"So here's my proposition,'' Callahan said, resting his hands on his knees and leaning forward. "There's twenty-five hundred head of prime steers out on my range, ready to be driven to market. I want you to ramrod 'em all the way to Abilene. You do that, you'll get twenty percent of the price for the surviving head of cattle. Straight off the top.''

Slocum felt his stomach turn over inside him. The J-Bar-C herd would bring two hundred fifty thousand dollars from the Frenchman. A quarter of a million dollars. And his share . . . fifty thousand.

Elianora laughed at the expression on his face.

"Why so much?'' Slocum asked when he could find his voice again.

"If all the steers make it, you get fifty grand, your men get fifty grand, and I get a hundred fifty. That's twice the normal price for a herd that size.'' He took a slug of his own whiskey. His sky-blue eyes glowed with excitement. "You won't get all the steers to market; you never do. But the proportions'll stay the same, however many make it.''

The whitewashed walls and heavy carved furniture of the room seemed to swim in Slocum's vision. Even if only half the steers survived to reach Abilene, he'd make twenty-five thousand dollars. It was vastly more than he'd ever even hoped to see at one time.

"But a trail boss usually don't make more'n ninety a month," he protested. Normally he wouldn't have thought twice; if a man was fool enough to throw his money away, and cared to throw a chunk of it in his direction, why, that was purely fine with John Slocum. But this was Joe Callahan, who was Slocum's friend and no kind of a fool at all.

Callahan eased himself back with a sigh. "You'll earn it, Johnny," he said in a voice surprisingly small to be coming out of that great barrel of a chest. "You'll earn it."

"But I told you, I ain't no cowhand!"

Slowly Callahan shook his head. "I got good hands who can go with you, take care of the herd and run it right. But I don't need a drover for trail boss. I need a man I can depend on. A hard man."

Seeing that Slocum still didn't understand, the big man took another taste of his drink and dropped his eyes to the flannel blanket that covered his lap, his withered useless legs. "My son had seen a lot of war by the time he took over your company, Johnny," he said quietly. "You were the best sergeant he ever knew. You took scared-green recruits and hammered them into soldiers who had a chance to survive out on the line. You never took more guff from a newly minted officer than an army mule, and never let 'em make the men miserable or waste their lives; but a good officer knew you'd see his orders carried out, solid as a rock. Men who didn't even give a damn for Secesh or the South would give their lives for you."

"That ain't true," Slocum said in a rough voice. "They gave 'em for Kevin. Not me."

But Callahan shook his head. "For Kevin, yes, but for you, too." He paused, drew a deep breath, shuddery, like a horse that had run itself plumb out. "Kevin loved you like a brother, Johnny. And you know, and I know, that most officers were a hell of a lot closer to their nigger slaves than to their own men in Jeff Davis's army. Yeah, Johnny, Kevin saw in you the brother he never had. But there was one thing he told me in his letters, Johnny. *There's no better man than John Slocum in this whole army*, he wrote, *but he does have him a real streak of mean*.

"That's why I'm hiring you to drive this herd to Abilene, John. You've got you a streak of mean."

She came to him in moonlight, her clean bright smell her only perfume.

At the sound of the door latch being lifted he came awake, an army Colt cocked and ready in his hand. Then he caught the shimmer of moonlight on sheer silk, silver highlights dancing on jet-black hair. He sighed and eased the hammer in with a click.

"You shouldn't come sneakin' in like that," he started to say. He never had the chance. Elianora Callahan crossed the room in a bound like a cat's and was on him, mouth pressed to his, tongue questing. For a moment his instinct for self-preservation shouted for him to pull back. What if Callahan came upon them? Would he shoot John Slocum where he lay for so abusing his hospitality?

And: Was it right to do this? his honor asked. Slocum was startled. That was a voice he hadn't heard in some time. He'd wondered if he'd ever hear it again.

But Elianora's hand was grasping, urging, drawing

forth a response he could not contain. Her full breasts were soft and sweet against his bare chest, the nipples hard. The aroused and urgent smell of her filled his nostrils like drugged smoke, intoxicating him like wine, like violence. With a moan he laid down his gun and reached for her.

Her gown fell open. Her skin was cool and dry and vibrant with youth and health and passion. He captured a breast with one hand, rolled the taut nipple between thumb and forefinger. She gasped and wrenched at the thin sheet, pulling aside the barrier between their naked bodies. Then she was straddling him, her cool strong legs on either side of him. She rose, tall, proud and alabaster in the moonlight, then settled slowly down onto him. He clenched his teeth as the tight cool wetness of her swallowed him up. Then she leaned forward, breasts swaying enticingly. Thought was forgotten, doubt and honor and apprehension, as those powerful velvet-skinned haunches began to churn.

For a time they strove together in silence and moonlight, the communion of mutual need. Outside a cloud drifted across the pocked half-face of the moon, and in the brief darkness an owl swept down and its claws found a scurrying gray field mouse that had been dining on hen scratch near the open bedroom window. The mouse's death cry, thin and pitiful, was echoed by a low and deep-throated cry from within as the woman's passion took her in its claws.

A moment more and Slocum spent himself in a mindless driving, his feet braced against the maple bedstead, his hands kneading her breasts and back. He subsided back into the sheets. They clung to him, sweat-soaked and chill, as his fervent caresses eased to a gentle stroking of the long, fine, muscular back.

He lay for a time unspeaking, enjoying the feeling of

satiety and the lazy warm weight of the woman sprawled atop him. Then apprehension began to gnaw at him again with tiny rat's teeth.

"You shouldn't have come," he said as she nuzzled his cheek.

He felt her stiffen briefly. "Are you going to tell me what I should or shouldn't do in my father's house? Or do you feel you've somehow dishonored my father?" She raised her head and looked down at him, her green eyes like flecks of brilliants in the glow of the moon that was beginning to slip below the ridge to the west.

He made himself meet her eyes. She'd hit uncomfortably near the mark, and that made him uneasy. "I'm a guest in this house," he said.

"This is my house as well as my father's," she said, shaking back her glossy black hair. "And as for me, I'm my own woman. My father doesn't own me."

Slocum said nothing. In a moment the tension left her. She eased herself back down, her cheek to his, and rubbed him gently. She seemed to like the raspy sound and feel of her skin against his nocturnal stubble of beard.

"My brother thought you were the finest man he'd met," she said. "How did he die, Johnny?"

Slocum looked up into the darkness among the *vigas* of the ceiling, seeing not formless black but a brush-covered hillside half a continent away, shrouded in smoke through which bright spikes of fire stabbed and sought like serpent's tongues. He had been a visitor at the J-Bar-C perhaps half a dozen times since the war ended, stopping by to see the father of his friend and comrade Kevin Callahan on his way from here to there, and never once had Joe Callahan inquired about the manner of his son's death. Nor had Kevin's younger sister Ellie.

But always before Ellie had been a girl, a gawky, uncertain, adolescent tomboy with her black hair wrapped in tight pigtails. In the three years since Slocum had last been in New Mexico Territory, the girl had become a beautiful, self-possessed young woman, who definitely had a mind of her own. Now she had asked to hear the painful story, and he was strangely unreluctant to tell her.

"I didn't see it," he said to the shadows of the ceiling. "I was lying in a hospital back in Gettysburg with a .44 ball in my belly. I got that the second day. We were with John Bell Hood's brigade, trying to turn the Yankees' southern flank on Cemetery Ridge. There was this little hill at the end of the ridge, a woody, rocky little thing that our scouts said didn't have nobody on it. We was to try to take the hill and just roll up the Yankees' flanks.

"Old John Hood, he wanted to just bypass the line and try to get in the bluecoats' rear. But Bobby Lee wouldn't let him. Wanted to do it by the book, and so that's how we did."

He lapsed into silence for a moment, breathing deep, eyes unfocused. Elianora eased herself off him to the side. He didn't seem to be answering her question, yet she sensed that he was. But he was speaking from his own need now, not hers, and she would hear him out.

"Our Texas boys went in with a regiment from Alabama, right at that round hill the scouts said wasn't defended. Only it was. Bunch of Yankee boys from Maine had occupied it before we moved out. We got cut to pieces." His eyes narrowed with the memory of pain. "Kevin led his boys right up to the rocks where the bluecoats was. A Yankee sergeant, big bearded buck with a cannonball belly on him, he let me have it spang in the belly with his Rogers and Spencer. Like bein' hit with a sledge."

He shook his head. Elianora toyed idly with the tight curled hair on his chest and waited. "Thought I was done for. Ever'thing went all red and black like, an' the next thing I know Kevin was carryin' me to the rear in his arms. Cryin' like a baby. The boys'd just broke and run—nothin' for it, there were dyin' there, never had a chance. But they'd never run before. Not ever. And Kevin knew they'd never be the same.

"Well, he got me on a ambulance and rode it back to Gettysburg with me. This doctor fella with a two days' growth of beard looks at me, lets out a long breath that couldn't't've been less'n ninety proof, and says, 'Belly wound—he'll never make it. Put him over there with the other goners.' "

Slocum glanced at the girl. She had not led a sheltered life, but the shock was plain in her eyes. "Kevin never batted an eye. He said, 'Surgeon, see to this man.' Surgeon said, 'I'll be damned if I will.' Kevin pulled his pistol and said he'd be damned a damned sight sooner if he didn't. So the surgeon operated on me, and took the ball out. Hadn't really pierced my guts after all, or I wouldn't be here today, just hit a rib and then lodged in muscle. But I couldn't walk. Kevin sat with me till late that night, then went back to the men."

He raised his hard, weathered hands to rub at his eyes. "Next day our company went in with Pickett. Kevin was right there in the front line. Made it all the way up to the Yankee lines before canister got him."

He heard the catch of her breath, felt sudden wetness on his chest. "I don't know how to tell it no better," he said hoarsely. "Sorry."

She took his hand in both of hers, shaking her head. "No. I wanted the truth, and you gave it to me." She kissed his hand.

He held her to him and stroked her hair until she

raised her head to smile at him with dry eyes. "It's a good thing you turned up when you did," she said. "Dad needed a good man to boss this drive for him."

"I don't know if it's such a good thing, Ellie. Don't know nothin' about drivin' cattle."

She hoisted herself on one elbow, looking down at him with her hair spilling in a dark torrent over her face. "You know how to lead, Johnny. You know how to lead men into danger and bring them out alive. That's what my father needs on this drive."

He laced his fingers behind his head and shook it to clear away the last fragments of image of the hospital at Gettysburg, with the screaming bloody wounded all around, the clouds of flies, the stink of gangrene and spilled guts, the ghastly gray-blue pile of severed arms and legs behind the tents through which hungry mongrels rooted despite the shouts and shots of sentries.

The horrible pictures were replaced by a golden vision. Fifty thousand dollars! He couldn't believe it, could scarcely even imagine it.

Normally he thought of money in terms of how best he could blow it on a high old time—high-stakes poker, free-flowing booze, and women, always women, painted and feathered and satiny and oh, so willing. And stone cold broke at the end of it, with his pockets turned inside out and his head ringing like an anvil. And the contemptuous stares of barkeeps and whores as he crept out to his horse. Nothing begins to stink quicker than a high roller who's shot his wad.

But the prospect of fifty thousand dollars forced him to think in a whole new way. That wasn't a couple hundred to be pissed away in a high wide old evening. It was an opportunity. A man could buy a lot for that kind of money. Land, a home, cattle to run—or horses, perhaps; Slocum was a Kentucky boy with fine horses in his blood. That kind of money could buy a man a way out of the life of a drifter, a permanently down-at-heels saddle tramp who would one day drop down dead in a ditch with never anyone to know or care. A chance to be *somebody*.

But no prize that grand and glorious ever came easy. John Slocum had been hammered around enough in his life to have that basic truth pounded into his skull. "Bein' a sergeant's one thing," he said slowly. "Bossin' a cattle drive's another. Hell, I never even been on one. Back in '66, when the big drives started, I was down in Mexico with Shelby, fighting the Frenchies for gold and Juarez."

She ran a finger down the hard ridges of his rib cage. "You hate the French, don't you."

"Yep." He didn't feel like discussing his reasons with her. She sensed that and didn't press him—a fact which made him uneasy for reasons he couldn't name. "That's another thing I don't like about this deal. I just don't trust the Frenchies. This colonel of your father's got some kind of treachery up his sleeve, don't ever doubt it."

"I thought the French were supposed to hold their honor in high regard."

He snorted. "Ellie, a Frenchman's like a lot of your fine Southern gentlemen. Honor's just the face he puts on doin' what he wants to do."

"My father says the French are liable to be in a bad way with this war. He says they won't have any choice but to deal squarely with us."

"Maybe—if it's a last resort. But I will put my faith in gold." He laughed. "Yeah, I won't even mind doin' the French a good turn, for a shot at fifty thousand."

"This means a lot to my father."

Still giddy with the promise of gold, he answered,

"Yes, ma'am, I'd certainly call one hundred fifty thousand dollars a lot. Just about enough, if there was any such thing," He laughed again. "Which there ain't."

"It's not just that," Ellie said, dead serious now. "My father's not a man who likes losing. And that's what he's been doing these last few years—losing. He's lost his wife, his only son, the use of his legs. He's only half a man now, he thinks, less than half. And it's killing him." She shook her head. "He needs one more big win in his life to prove that everything up until the war wasn't just a fluke. He needs to feel he can leave something big when he leaves this life, since he doesn't have a son to carry on the line." Momentary bitterness clogged her throat, then she went on. "That's why it's providential you showed up, Johnny. Because you can do it. If any man can get this herd to Abilene, you can."

"But, damn it, Ellie, I don't know nothin' about cows!"

She smiled. "But father's got some good hands to send along with you. They know all about it."

"Well they sure-hell won't listen to no greenhorn like me then!"

"Oh, but they will," she said, grinning broadly now. "Daddy's sending someone along with you who knows as much about running beeves as any of them, and who they'll be sure to listen to."

He raised his head. "Yeah, and who's that?"

Ellie Callahan moistened her lips and nibbled briefly at the lobe of his ear before whispering, "Me."

3

"John," the chunky gray-blond wrangler said. "Miss Ellie's askin' for you to come over to the wagon. That sodbuster boy done woke up."

John Slocum sopped up the last remnants of his beans with a shred of blue-corn tortilla and stood. Hunkered around the coffeepot simmering on a low cow-chip fire, the men stopped eating for a moment to look sidelong at Slocum.

"Tell her I'll be there in a minute."

He could feel their eyes on him as he walked down to the stream to rinse out his tin plate. The water had begun to run clear again; the mud raised by the crossing of twenty-five hundred steers had finally settled out. It had taken all afternoon to get the herd across—a long delay, but expected. So far the drove was running slightly ahead of schedule.

They'd made good time so far. From the northeast corner of New Mexico through the narrow panhandle of Indian Territory to this stream in the lower southwestern edge of Kansas had cost them two weeks. They'd had good weather and better luck, and by phenomenal good chance the chief of the Comanche band that they encountered soon after crossing out of Texas was an old acquaintance of Slocum's; they'd been able to buy safe passage across the territory for only a nominally extortionate price. For a week now the old hands in the crew had been shaking their heads in wonder and saying they'd never known such a smooth-running drive, nor heard tell of one.

Squatting down by the murmuring water, Slocum gazed across at the south bank of the stream through the softly dying light. They'd gotten happy, lazy, and complacent. And young Jimmie Fitzhugh had gotten dead. *Well, at least I won't have no trouble keeping the men sharp from here on in*, Slocum thought.

The sleeves of Ellie's bleached linen shirt were rolled up around her elbows and her hair was drawn back in a severe bun. She smelled of dust and sweat, and her fine cheek was smudged with dirt, and she looked as desirable as any woman Slocum had ever seen.

Reining in the hunger that stirred in the pit of his belly, he said, "Dane said you wanted to see me."

She rubbed at her forehead with the back of her hand. From the other side of the wagon came the smell of boiling beans and Cookie singing to himself in his thunderbass rumble. "The boy woke up. He's slightly feverish and keeps calling for his father."

"Can he talk?"

Anger flared up briefly in her eyes. Then she nodded. "I think so."

Slocum waited for her to protest his bothering the wounded boy, but instead she simply stood by, waiting. It was clear that she understood the necessity of speaking to him now, even if he was in pain. Once more Slocum felt an uneasiness in him that had come to be a fairly constant companion in the last few weeks. He wasn't used to that sort of hardheaded practical understanding from a woman.

The chuck wagon had been driven across first, since the heavily laden canvas-covered vehicle would certainly have bogged had it tried to cross the stream after its soft mud bottom had been churned by ten thousand sharp hooves. The wounded boy had ridden across on a makeshift pallet of flour sacks arranged atop barrels of coffee, and once the wagon was parked on the northern bank Cookie had consented with the scowling ill grace that was his response to every request to let the men move some barrels out of the way and arrange a more comfortable bed. Some of the men had grumbled at taking this trouble over the "low-down skunk who'd shot Jimmie." A few sharp words from Ellie had silenced them, but even now Slocum could feel their eyes on him from around the campfire.

Slocum boosted himself onto the tailgate of the wagon. At the thump of his boot heel the boy shifted beneath his worn army blanket. "Pa?"

Bent low beneath the iron hoops that held the wagon's canvas cover, Slocum came forward, stepping lightly. He knelt down beside the boy. "Nope," he said.

The boy opened his eyes. They burned a bright, fevered blue. Immediately they widened with fright. "You're the man who shot me!"

Slocum nodded. "You was shootin' at me," he said. "You killed one of my men. A good man. Never gave him a chance." He shook his head. "He was a feller not much older'n yourself."

The boy shut his eyes. "We had to keep you out of our country," he said. "Your steers'll trample our crops and make our cattle sicken up and die with that Texas fever."

"These're clean beeves, son. And we're in the zone the legislature set aside for Texas drives. We ain't gonna disturb your crops or nothin' else. All we want is to get these steers to market. You had no call to bushwhack us."

He felt the wagon shift on its springs, and caught the scent of Ellie, knew she had climbed in after him. He had no chance to glance back. The boy reared up from his pallet. "That's a lie! You're all the same! You're just like the last bunch. They said there'd be more of their murdering kind along, and they was right!"

Slocum felt a thrill of alarm run down his back. "The last bunch?" he asked gruffly. "Who you talkin' about, boy?"

"Drovers from Texas," the boy said. "Just like you." Quick as a snake he drew back his head and spat full in Slocum's face. *"Murdering scum!"*

Ellie tensed. Slocum pulled a red handkerchief from his back pocket, easy-like, and mopped at his face. "Easy, boy, easy," he said. "Who was these people, and when did they come through?"

The boy's arms, locked trembling tight in fury to hold him up, suddenly gave way and he fell back with a sob of anger. A fresh spot of red appeared beside the rust-brown stains on the bandages wrapped about his chest. Ellie sucked in a breath through her teeth but said nothing. She too had read the import in the boy's words.

With the reopening of the wound the fight flowed out of the boy, and bitter tears cascaded down his cheek. "Came through a week ago. Like some plague out of the Bible, they was. Right out of the south. Drove their herd right through our fields, never looked left or right. Whenever they passed a homestead they just took what they wanted. Sam Cassidy tried to stop them cleanin' him out, they just shot him through the belly and left him to die. Camped right outside town, and when they heard the marshal was plannin' to arrest the guilty ones they came and horsewhipped him in front of the jail. Said that'd be the lot of any man tried to stand in their way. Said they was aimin' to get their herd to Abilene afore anybody else, and get this big bounty some foreigner was payin' for beef on the hoof, and nobody was gonna stop 'em—God, man, or the Devil himself.''

Slocum glanced at Ellie. A cold fire burned in his steel-gray eyes. "Who said this, boy?'' he rasped.

"Their leader. Young feller. Had—'' He coughed. Ellie started forward and Slocum restrained her with a raised hand. "Had real gold-yeller hair and a face like a angel. Said his name was Billy Land, Lance—something like that.

"Lancer.'' The word slipped out between Slocum's clenched teeth.

The boy didn't hear. The tears started again, heavier than before. "Then just before they left, my sis went into town. They—they took her. Did all sorts of horrible things to her and just left her lay out on the prairie when they rode out. Pa was gone off to the county seat, and came riding back and found her out there that morning, all bruised-up and bleeding and cryin' fit to die. He . . . he swore he'd die rather than let another Texas drive cross his land. And now he's dead. And you killed him!''

He tried to rise, to fling himself on Slocum. Ellie pushed by the man to put her hands on the boy's shoulders and force him gently back. He fought for a moment, then turned to her and buried his head against her chest, sobbing uncontrollably. She hugged him, murmured to him. Slocum sidled past her and duck-walked out of the wagon.

He took his bag of Bull Durham out of his pocket and rolled himself a smoke. The sun sank into a bank of leaden clouds lying heavily on the western horizon, casting a watery gray light over the flat prairie, the slow-rolling stream, the humped and huddled shapes of the longhorns as they settled themselves down for the night under the watchful eyes of a handful of mounted drovers.

He heard the scrape of Ellie's high boot heels and she sprang lithely down beside him. "Shit," he said, not caring that she heard.

"He's asleep now."

"Will he make it?"

"Your bullet broke two ribs and came out under his right arm. He hasn't spit up any blood, so I don't think there's any internal damage. He's young. He should pull through." She washed her hands with the damp cloth she'd been using to mop the boy's brow and leaned exhaustedly against the tailgate. "Now is when it gets bad, isn't it?"

He nodded.

She reached up and untied the ribbon that held her hair, shook it free with the wanton joy of a foal released from its stall. "We'll have to fight our way from here," she said. Eagerness edged her voice, it seemed to Slocum. She looked up at him. "The way you charged that ambush—was that the right thing to do? It was so dangerous."

He spat out a fragment of tobacco. "Wasn't, particularly. That's usually the only thing to do, you get caught out in the open like that. Just charge straight into the ambush. If the 'bushers is inexperienced, like these was, they commonly run when they see they ain't got you buffaloed."

"And if they don't?"

He laughed.

She ran slim fingers carelessly through her hair. "But these did, didn't they." She shook her head and laughed too. "John Slocum, you ride awfully close to the edge."

He made himself keep his eyes from her. She was ripe

and vital and womanly. She'd never led a sheltered life, but these two weeks on the trail had polished her, trimming her body to perfection, the sun giving a darkness to her face and a luster to her hair that made her eyes glow like emeralds. He ached from wanting her, now more than usual. He wanted to cleanse the day's violence and the boy's story from his mind in the fury of lovemaking. But he was starkly aware of Cookie's gruff humming from the other side of the wagon, aware that the men were watching surreptitiously. They'd been without women themselves for two weeks now, and had a long dry stretch before them if Kansas proved out as hostile as their welcome indicated. Any open display of affection between Slocum and Joe Callahan's lovely daughter could lead to an eruption of jealousy—a lethal one, perhaps.

He'd fought hard to keep her from coming. To his utter disbelief Callahan had offered no resistance to the notion. "She knows cows and the men know her," he said. "She can give you all the backing you need."

"But she's just a girl!" Slocum had protested.

Callahan shook his massive head. "She's run this ranch since . . . since my accident. She was still in pigtails then, but she went at it hard all the same. No man could have worked harder. She's got as big a stake in this as I do, Johnny boy. I can't keep her back."

Slocum couldn't help but feel there was more to the story than that. But Callahan was the boss. For the chance the man was giving him, Slocum could only do as Callahan asked in the matter.

And he had to admit there were many times in the last two weeks he'd been glad Ellie was along. There were a hundred details of herding that were as strange to him as the backside of the moon, but Ellie was always there to point out what had to be done. Without her he'd have been lost.

He was also glad of her presence on those too rare nights when they could slip away from the camp together for a brief time, for hot bouts of lovemaking with nothing but the starry sky to cover their grappling hungry bodies. He was riding near the edge to do that, too, he knew. But he couldn't keep himself from her. God knew how hard it was for him to keep his hands off now.

But today he hadn't been glad to have her along. If the sodbusters hadn't run she might have been shot. And if anything happened to Ellie, even her father would forgive him long before John Slocum forgave himself.

"What are you going to do with the boy?" she asked, a little apprehensively.

"Take him back to his people."

She sighed relief. "It'll be hard for him, with his father gone."

"He's a brave kid. He stood his ground and took a shot at me after I killed his pa. He'll get by."

The sun sank into the clouds. He took a few more drags on his cigarette, crushed it out, and stuck the butt end in his pocket, an unconscious action born both of habitual poverty and the frequent need to travel overland while leaving no sign of passage.

"What—what the boy said, about the other drive," she said at length, her face averted. "They're going after Colonel LeBlanc's bounty too, aren't they."

He nodded, keeping his eyes on the horizon. The notion that her father had been wrong to trust the Frenchman agonized her, and he didn't want to embarrass her by looking. "You seemed to know the name he told you," she said. "Who is it?"

His lip curled. "Lancer. Billy Lancer." He spat to clear the taste of the name from his mouth. "Lowest backshooter that ever crawled the earth. Deserted from both armies back during the war. Got thrown out of Quantrill's *guerrilleros* because he was too damn killing crazy—and Quantrill was no soft man. He'd steal a widow's last crust of bread and shoot his best friend in the back because he liked the way his horse stepped out. Matter of fact, he did." He shook his head. "Face like an angel, blond hair like a halo. Kid described him real well. But if he ain't the Devil himself, he'll do till a better model turns up."

"Why would anyone hire him to drive his herd to railhead?"

"Same reason your daddy hired me, Ellie. Wanted him a hard man to ramrod the drove through. But he got hisself a mad dog instead."

"What'll we do?"

"Keep drivin' for Abilene and keep our eyes open."

"You won't do anything to this Billy Lancer?"

Reluctantly Slocum shook his head. "Your daddy told us to steer clear of trouble, and Billy Lancer's trouble on the hoof." He rubbed at the wiry stubble on his chin. "I'd purely love to be the man to bury Billy Lancer. What he did to that boy's sister is kind of a callin' card of his. But if he keeps clear of us we won't go lookin'."

He started back toward the campfire. "Will he?" Ellie asked.

He paused for a moment. "No way in hell," he said, and walked on.

The night had come down full dark except for a sullen red glow along the top of the band of clouds in the west when Slocum returned to the campfire. His men had mostly finished eating and were sitting around smoking and trading lies. The slangy, drawling conversation ebbed as he resumed his place in the circle.

Cord Blaylock eyed him across the flames. "What d'you aim to do with that sodbuster brat?" he asked.

"We got ourselves all kinda rope," piped up the thin, rat-faced man who sat beside the lean Tennessean. "We could give him a nice horsehair necktie."

All other conversation had stopped by now. The men's eyes shifted from Slocum to Blaylock and back again. John Slocum may have known little enough of cattle, but he was a keen judge of men. He'd spotted Cord Blaylock as a troublemaker from the outset. Left to himself he would have left Blaylock back in Mora County, but as with Ellie, he'd had little choice. Callahan could only spare a half-dozen men for the drive, and there was no way to run a drove this big all the way to Abilene with that few men. Callahan had scraped together enough men who were known to be competent with beeves—and guns—to make a go of it by the time John Slocum had dropped out of the blue onto the J-Bar-C. But the rancher didn't know many of the ones who weren't his own hands personally, and he'd had to take a chance on the reliability of the new drovers.

Not that Blaylock, or his little sharp-featured black-haired friend Bob Ed Bogen, had given any overt trouble since the drive left the J-Bar-C. Blaylock did know cattle and cattle drives, could ride that big white-stocking stud as if grafted to its back, and the campfire gossip said he could use the two war-vintage Shawk & McLanahan sixguns he wore at his hips well enough that few men ever trifled with him more than once. He'd been on one of the fateful drives into Kansas in 1866, and that drive had taken fewer losses in beeves—and men—than many another. Little Bob Ed was never far from his side, and seemed to handle the steers well enough. Whether he was any use in a fight there was no knowing. All Slocum knew about him was that he'd be mighty wary of calling Cord Blaylock out if Bob Ed Bogen was standing behind Slocum's back.

But there were the constant comments, some blared by Blaylock, some whispered aside by Bob Ed, picking at Slocum, running him down. Slocum had ignored them, knowing full he couldn't stop the men from talking, and understanding that he'd be giving in to Blaylock if he tried. But since he'd gunned down the fleeing farmer that afternoon, Blaylock had been arching his neck and strutting like a young stud who was of a mind to challenge the boss stallion.

The other men knew it too. They leaned forward without seeming to, eyes aglitter in the firelight, ears cocked to catch every nuance of every syllable that passed between the antagonists. "I'm taking him back to his people tomorrow," he said quietly.

Bob Ed uttered a whinny of disbelief and derision.

"Well, if that don't beat damn all," drawled Blaylock. "I go to the trouble of gunning down some shit-heel farmer to keep him from bringing all his friends down on our necks. And now you want to go and spread the word for him." He shook his head.

"And what about that damned kid!" screeched Bogen. "He shot poor Jimmie in cold blood! I ain't forgot, even iffen you have." He looked around at the others, eyes shining like black glass beads. "Or maybe your feet are getting just a mite chilly, Slocum? You maybe wanna try to weasel in good with these sodbusters, save yourself some trouble? Are you maybe just a little teensy bit *scared*?"

Every muscle in Slocum's body snapped taut at the

last word. He'd always hated men who could only keep discipline at gunpoint. But he couldn't let this little rat of a man as much as call him a coward and expect to keep the respect of these hard-bitten Texas and New Mexico drovers. He started to get to his feet, noticing as he did that Blaylock eased a hand back to rest on a pistol butt.

"This is something I don't understand, señores." A voice spoke from the darkness past Slocum's shoulder. "I have spoken the English since I was quite small, but this I'm afraid you must explain, *por favor*."

He sauntered forward into the circle of firelight, a slender man of medium height, showing white teeth through his *bandido* mustache in a shy grin, his thumbs hooked through the broad silver-chased gunbelt that upheld his brace of Colt Dragoons. The men looked at him with grins of their own, knowing as well as Slocum did that when Santiago Velarde spoke in that accent he did so with his tongue planted firmly in his cheek. He was one of Callahan's hands, and popular even though he was a Mexican.

"You say you think maybe Señor Slocum is scared. Now I thought *scared* meant, you know, frightened, afraid. But I saw him ride right up into the muzzles of the ambushers' guns this afternoon. So this is very brave, and so I know a smart man like you cannot mean he's afraid. So I'm confused." He struck himself on the forehead. "*Caramba*! This English! Or maybe I'm just a stupid Mexican. You explain it to me, please, Señor Bogen?"

Bob Ed went purple and his thin lips curled in an angry snarl. The circle of men around the fire broke into loud guffaws. The little wrangler looked as if he were about to leap to his feet, but Blaylock touched him on the arm and muttered something to him. His face drained of color as he stared furiously at the Mexican, but he kept his place.

"The sodbusters think they have to defend their farms against us," Slocum said loudly across the heavy laughter. From the corner of his eye he noticed how Velarde's hands had slipped casually back on his hips, into easy reach of the outsized pistols. "Looks like we ain't the only drove bound for Abilene."

Velarde's intervention having broken the tension of a moment before, everyone turned to Slocum to hear the story he'd gotten from the injured boy. At the name Lancer a murmur of concern ran around the campfire, and even Cord Blaylock lost some of his shine. The few men who hadn't heard of Lancer before turned puzzled expressions to the others. Billy Lancer's colorful career would provide enough substance for yarns to keep the men busy until it was time to turn in, so Slocum excused himself and went to check on the men on watch over the bedded-down drove.

He was hunkered down on the stream bank, smoking and listening to the water, enjoying the coolness after the sweltering heat of the day, when he heard the soft crackling of summer-dry grass beneath boot leather. He dropped his right hand to his Colt but didn't turn. "Ellie?"

A low chuckle answered him. "I know what is on your mind, señor. Difficult not to think of that one, ¿qué no?"

Slocum plucked his cigarette from his mouth with his left hand, scowled at it a moment, and flicked it into the water. It died with a brief hiss. "Don't see as how it's any concern of yours, what I'm thinkin'."

Yellow light flared as Velarde scratched a lucifer alight. "No, of course not. A man's thoughts are private." He was standing next to Slocum now, lighting one of his thin black *cigarillos*. Slocum saw the glint of white teeth in the brief glow of the match.

"That Señor Bogen," Velarde said. "He reminds me of the dogs in the little village where I grew up. They'd snarl and show their teeth at you, and run away if you lifted a fist. But the Virgin of Guadalupe help you if they caught you with your back turned!" He blew a long streamer of smoke. "That Blaylock, though. He's a different sort of animal. A big gray *lobo*, perhaps."

Slocum uncoiled till he was towering over the Mexican. "I got a proposition for your, *señor*," he said, coming down heavy on the final word. "You just worry about them steers, and leave Blaylock to me."

The firefly glow of Velarde's cigarillo bobbed up and down. "As you wish." Behind them they heard the heavy footfalls of a wandering steer, then the drum of a hoofbeats as a drover headed him off and chivvied him back to the herd with clucks and low cries.

"You saw those clouds in the west when the sun went down, señor?" Velarde asked. Slocum nodded. "It's getting to be the stormy season. What look like simple harmless clouds can pile up into thunderheads *muy pronto*, my friend. Before you know it."

With an effort Slocum kept from snarling back that he wasn't friend to any Mexican. He hadn't missed the import of Velarde's words. He turned away and started to walk back toward the orange dance of the campfire.

"Oh, Señor Slocum." He stopped. "If you go the other direction, it may be you'll find someone waiting for you just beyond the rise." And whistling brightly he walked past Slocum toward the camp.

4

The morning sun was already stinging hot and had bleached the eastern sky like old blue flannel when the lone rider appeared on the edge of town. His paint pony's hooves stirred up little dispirited swirls of red dust as he rode down the main street. Its head hung low, and its ears were lopped down to the sides in protest at being forced to carry an unaccustomed burden in this lead-heavy, humid heat.

The indolent appraisal of the newcomer by a trio of loafers on the boardwalk in front of the general store turned to agitation as the townies saw that the tall hard-eyed stranger wasn't alone. "Hey!" yelled one old codger with a grizzled beard furring both skinny cheeks. "Ain't that young George Martin ahind that feller?" His straight-backed chair, which he'd had tipped back against the weathered slats of the store, thumped forward. One of the legs caught the tail of the old yellow mongrel curled at his feet. With a yelp the animal jumped to its feet and, giving the oldster a reproachful look, trotted off down the street. Instinctively it gave the newcomer a wide berth; it hadn't got to be an old hound by being a foolish one.

An apple-cheeked man with a fringe of white hair around the base of his shiny-domed skull bustled out of the store, wiping his hands on his apron. "Yah? Vot's dis?"

"If there's a doctor in town you better fetch him," John Slocum said. "This boy's hurt."

"I'll fetch him, Swede," said the oldster who'd winged the dog. After an appraising look at Slocum, he added, "Maybe I best fetch the marshal, as well." He took off up the street at an odd banty-cock walk, elbows high and pumping at his sides.

At Slocum's back the boy moaned. Ellie hadn't wanted to let her patient go, but Slocum pointed out that the kid could get a lot better care in town—unless she wanted to hold up the herd for a few days while he recuperated. Her heart wasn't that soft; and besides, the town wasn't too far away. A ride of a few miles wouldn't do the boy much damage.

"Hold on a few minutes, son," he muttered to the boy. In a few moments he heard a commotion up the street from the direction the loafer had gone, and saw a knot of men hurrying toward him. A white-whiskered sandhill crane of a man strode in the lead, black coat-tails flapping, a black leather bag in his hand. "You the doc?" Slocum called as the crowd drew near.

The crane halted and poked a pair of square-rimmed specs higher up on his beak. "Why, um, yes, I'm Dr. Gage—"

"Good. This here boy's been shot. Needs medical attention bad. You two"—he nodded at two of the crane's followers—"help him off this horse."

The townsmen hastened to obey the stranger's top-sergeant commands. "Huh—who're you?" the doctor asked as the boy was lifted down.

"What's goin' on here?" a new voice called from behind Slocum. The tall man turned in the saddle. A heavyset man was approaching from the other direction, limping along heavily with the aid of a cane. One eye looked out of a socket filled to overflowing by a purple bruise. A sawed-off double shotgun was tucked under one arm, and a five-pointed metal star glinted dully from the breast of the man's frock coat. "What happened to the boy?"

The doctor, bent down over the boy, who had been lowered onto the porch of the store, uttered a startled exclamation. "My heavens! He's been shot!"

The marshal turned a hard look at Slocum. "That's right," Slocum said levelly. "I shot him."

A gasp rose from the onlookers. Slocum left his eyes on the marshal's face. He sat easily in his saddle, relaxed and self-possessed.

The marshal's battered face grew bleak. "What you're sayin's mighty serious, mister."

"Yep," Slocum agreed with a slow nod. "It is. This boy here was a member of a party that shot one of my men from ambush and killed him. I don't aim to cause him no trouble by preferring charges of murder."

The marshal looked around at the crowd. "What do you-all know about this?"

The assembled men shifted from foot to foot and eyed each other nervously. "Well," said a gangly gotcheyed man in raggedy-ended trousers, "Sy Martin and Hiram Potts said they wasn't gonna take it lyin' down if that Billy Lancer's friends come hoo'rawin' through. After whut happent to Sy's daughter, an' all."

Slocum turned his steel-colored gaze to the man and drilled it into him hard. "Folks don't generally name me Billy Lancer's friend, mister. And they never do it twice." The man's prominent Adam's apple rose and fell apprehensively. Slocum turned back to the marshal.

"My herd's clean, and it ain't trampled nobody's crops all the way from New Mexico Territory. And my men don't do no hoo-rawin'. We'll mind our manners and keep to the zone the legislature set aside for Texas drives. But if anybody else tries to stop us against all law and justice, then God help that man." He smiled and reached up to lift the sun-faded brim of his Stetson. "Good day to you, Marshal. I hope the kid pulls through. He's going to be the man of the house from here on in."

In sullen silence the crowd watched him ride away up the red street and out of town.

Deeper into Kansas they penetrated, making good time, the herd rolling onward with the inevitability of an avalanche, seemingly unstoppable. When the settlers in and around the village where Slocum had left the boy offered no further hindrance to the passage of the drive, the men quickly forgot their initial resentment toward Slocum for Jimmie Fitzhugh's death, and likewise for his treatment of a party who had caused or helped to cause it. Abilene no longer seemed unimaginably remote. Though it was still several hundred miles and weeks of hard travel ahead, the drovers began to talk about what they'd do when they got there, spending in advance the fortunes a successful drive would bring them. Even Cord Blaylock and his hound-dog Bogen gave off trying to undermine Slocum's position with the men. But he knew better than to trust that pair, and likewise knew that any setback would cause the good-will the men bore him to evaporate like water tossed on a hot stove.

For five days the great herd hurdled on unimpeded. Nothing moved in the vast emptiness of the Kansas landscape, nothing but the dry stalks of bluestem and eddies of red dust tossed up by the questing wind, and sometimes birds, hawks floating high and lonely on unseen currents overhead, quail scurrying along the ground in their curious zigzag run. Heat from two sources burned John Slocum on those hard-driving days: the sun and Ellie.

Her body was a white flame of moonlight in the night, glistening with water droplets from a bath in a stream or from the sweat of exertion, long legs clamping, breasts swaying, black hair flying every which way as she cried out in passion and in need. In the light of day she was all business, taking a turn riding every position on the great seething herd—point, swing, flank, and even drag. In spite of Slocum's objections she even rode lead, way out in advance of the herd, the position traditionally taken by the trail boss and the one Jimmie Fitzhugh had been riding when he was shot. But there was no arguing with her, and Slocum couldn't deny that she did her share and more as well as any man. Her defiance made his hunger for her all the more fierce— and at the same time scared him. He didn't know if he was ready for a woman to do to him what Ellie did. There were times when he thought, *someday* . . . But he made his vision of someday-to-come focus on arriving in Abilene and claiming his fortune. Enough time after that, with unimagined wealth weighing down his saddle-bags, to tend to the somedays beyond.

Ever since the day of the ambush Slocum had ordered that two men should ride in the lead or scout position. He felt that would reduce the chance of the lead riders being taken by surprise—and that if they were, one would have a better chance of reporting back to the others. Back in the army they'd had a saying: A dead scout's a good scout. It meant that an enemy would give away his position by taking out a scout. It ran through

John Slocum's mind in an uncomfortable refrain whenever Ellie rode that position, sitting high in her saddle with her black hair caught in a bun or streaming free behind her in the breeze.

The fifth day from the ambush Slocum was back at point when he saw Velarde's red bay mare crest the long slow rise ahead at a gallop, making for the herd. The Mexican sat his saddle as he always did, in a way both indolent and proud, as if nothing in the world could hurry him, but the mare was eating up the ground. A sergeant's instinct made Slocum bark the orders to begin the ponderous process of bringing the herd to a halt before he spurred his scrubby paint forward to meet the other.

"Where's Lafe?" he demanded as he came into earshot. From behind rose the calls of the drovers as they went expertly about the trickish business of stopping the drove without causing the steers to mill. If the animals began to jostle and crowd each other too much, they started a churning commotion, milling, that was the prelude to every cowhand's nightmare: stampede. Slocum heard Ellie's voice pealing out above the rest, calm yet commanding, and he knew with a swell of pride that with her in charge there was nothing to fear.

The bay tossed her head as Velarde reined her in. "Carrihew's on the other side of the hill," he said. There was no trace of the thick greaseball accent he affected at times in his words, only business. "We spotted dust ahead, coming this way. About twenty riders, I'd say."

Slocum grunted skeptically. His estimate of Mexicans was never high, and even white men who were unaccustomed to battle tended to overestimate the number of potential enemies. "You think they mean to meet up with us?" he asked.

Laughing, Velarde nodded his head back at the herd. Though the hundreds of animals had mostly come to a halt and begun to crop at the grass, the dust they'd raised in their passage still loomed like a red column above them. With the uncomfortable feeling the Mexican had bested him again, Slocum nodded and said, "Who does Lafe think it is?"

"You and I both know who it is, señor," Velarde said. "Jayhawkers."

For all his experience, Slocum felt his gut tighten at the word. *Jayhawkers.* Yes. He knew.

"Get back to Lafe. Keep an eye on their dust. If it shows they're trying to flank us, let me know. Or if anybody shows hisself."

Velarde nodded and wheeled the horse. His lazy ease was gone. He bent down over the horse's neck and fairly flew up the slope.

Only a fear of spooking the steers kept Slocum from likewise sending his pony flat-out back to the drove. Ellie had been point rider on the other side of the herd. Her high-spirited chestnut stud was drawn up beside Cookie Cantwell's wagon, pawing the earth in impatience. "What's going on?" she called.

"We've got trouble," he called back. "Pass the word for the men to gather round, pronto."

Slocum had known independent-minded women before. To a one they'd have stood their ground, nostrils flaring and eyes flashing, at being ordered around in such a peremptory fashion. Not Ellie. She spun her horse around and loped off to obey without an instant's hesitation. He nodded in satisfaction. Then he read the feeling that welled within him and cursed out loud.

In a matter of seconds the drovers were gathered around the chuck wagon. They stayed mounted, with one eye always on the herd. "Trouble?" asked a slender black-haired man, brushing dust from his luxurious black mustache. Despite the hardships of the trail, Lonesome Dave Shapp always managed to be elegant, and the blued metal of his Colts gleamed as though freshly polished.

"Lafe and Velarde spotted riders, headed this way."

"Only one thing that could be," said Ray Polder, stroking his scrawny neck. The others looked at the old J-Bar-C wrangler. "Damned ruffians."

One or two looked puzzled. "Jayhawkers," Slocum rapped, and they nodded understanding. Hands went unconsciously to pistols, and eyes began to scan the surrounding horizon.

Being a veteran of the Yankee army, Ray Polder thought of them as border ruffians; to old Confederate John Slocum they were jayhawkers. In any man's terms they were trouble. Long before the War of Secession broke out, a state of war had existed in Kansas, a savage war that knew neither quarter nor neutrality. From Missouri came the bands of pro-slavery killers called border ruffians; fighting back were abolitionist gangs who called themselves jayhawkers. Both groups considered themselves guerrillas and heroes. Actually there was little to distinguish them from bandits. Most of them fought on through the war, Jennison and his jayhawkers for the Union, the ruffians most notably under command of Quantrill.

After the surrender at Appomattox a lot of the *guerrilleros* found it difficult to return to a placid peacetime existence. As a matter of grim fact, a good many found they had a lot more in common with their erstwhile blood enemies than with the civilian farmers and shopkeepers among whom they were now expected to take their places. At the core, most of them had ridden for the loot and the bloodshed first, and some ideal of abolition or slaveholders' rights second. So the former foes joined together in bandit gangs to continue what they'd really been up to for the better part of a decade: preying on their fellow man.

The great Texas drives of '66 had given them an excuse to portray themselves as selfless defenders of Kansan soil once again, robbing and murdering cattlemen under the pretext of trying to fend off the deadly Texas fever. Now the Texas fever scare was back, and so were the jayhawkers.

"So what do we do?" asked young Doug Travis, grinning with eagerness. If the skinny, blond-haired kid had had a tail he'd have wagged it. At his side his husky pal Charlie McBride nodded, seconding Doug's excitement in his calmer way. "Do we fight them? Charlie 'n' me'll show 'em a thing or two!"

Coming to a snap decision, Slocum said, "Nope. Charlie and you will stay with the herd. I want the rest of you up on the ridge line. Those that ain't got long guns, get 'em from Cookie."

The two boys' faces fell. But Slocum knew he'd done right. Though both were under twenty, the pair of them had grown up around cattle. Their hands with steers were as sure as any man's—and a sight surer than Slocum's, he had to admit ruefully. What he needed up on the ridge had nothing to do with droving. He needed older men, men who had seen the elephant—men who were likely to be able to face up to an enemy when the bullets flew. Because John Slocum knew, without a shadow of a doubt, that he and his men were about to fight for the herd—and the fortune that herd meant to every one of them.

Whistling and shaking his reins, Cookie had already urged his mules into grudging motion up the gentle slope. Ellie's chestnut trotted alongside. Slocum scowled and kneed his pony to a lope till he was beside her. "Where do you think you're goin'?" he demanded. "Git back to the herd."

"Doug and Charlie can manage by themselves."

"That ain't what I meant! There's liable to be shooting, and I don't aim to have you nowhere around."

Her fine-boned face went taut and white and turned forward, resolutely away. "Ellie, it ain't a woman's place to put herself in danger."

High spots of color burning on her cheeks, she rounded on him. "My place is helping defend my father's herd!" she cried. She drew her Winchester from its scabbard and brandished it like a saber. "Don't try to stop me, John Slocum!" Before he could say another word she spurred away from him, toward the crest of the hill.

His first impulse was to go after and force her to go back—hogtie her and throw her over the stallion's saddle if he had to. But he knew better than to try. She was every inch Joe Callahan's daughter right now. If he tried to get in her way she just might give him a bullet in the belly.

The wagon halted well down from the crest of the hill, turned sideways to the slope so as not to roll back. Cookie disappeared inside, to let down the tailgate a moment later and start bundling out long crates in his burly black-furred arms. Dane Andersen and a heavyset younger man named Shag Coltrane set the crates on the ground and broke them open with a prybar. Inside were long gleaming rifles, U.S. government-issue Springfield-Allin breechloaders. While they did not shoot as fast as repeaters, Slocum's Henry or Ellie's Winchester 66 or White Eyes Merriman's Spencer, they fired the latest .50-caliber center-fire cartridges at a fairly respectable rate, and hit a lot harder than the lever-actions. Before the drove had left New Mexico Territory, Slocum had made sure those men who lacked long arms of their own knew how to operate the breech-loading actions of the weapons. He hoped that with the five repeaters in the party they'd have firepower enough to deal with the jayhawkers.

A cry from the ridge line made Slocum turn. Velarde had appeared against the pale blue sky, waving his hand. "Riders, señor."

Slocum went up the incline as fast as the paint could carry him. Velarde awaited on horseback, Henry in hand. Lafe Carrihew, a hard-eyed hombre from Silver City who was rumored to have killed half a dozen men in gunfights, had his own repeater in hand and was squinting warily into the north.

From the ridge top the land fell gently away, much as it did to the south, before beginning yet another slow-swelling rise to a grass-clad crest line four or five hundred yards away. Down that far slope came a handful of riders, five by Slocum's count. So much for Velarde's estimate of their number, he thought, not without satisfaction.

"There're more of them behind the hill," said Carrihew, as if reading Slocum's mind. He was a tall, wolf-lean party with a deep trail tan and black-brown hair that was going to gray at the temples, though he was Slocum's own age. "The wind's out of the north. I heard a horse call from behind that ridge just after those buckos appeared."

Slocum's cheeks tightened in a grimace. The jayhawkers were leaving men out of sight—most of them, likely as not. *Damn that greaser*, he thought. *Looks like he's right again*.

"Dismount," he called back over his shoulder to his men. "Spread out along the ridge."

"Like hell I will!" Cord Blaylock's voice rang with outrage.

"What the hell you think we are, Slocum?" jeered Bob Ed Bogen. "Sodbusters? Do what you like. We're fightin' like men—on horseback."

White with fury, Slocum turned on them, drawing his Henry from the scabbard and cranking a round into the chamber. "You'll fight like I tell you," he snarled. "Or by God you'll leave your bones for the buzzards here!"

The repeater pointed midway between Blaylock and Bogen. Bogen's pale face went paler beneath the blue-white stubble of his beard. Blaylock licked his lips. His eyes visibly calculated his chances.

"Don't be an idiot, Blaylock," Shag Coltrane said in his quiet voice. "Do like he says."

Face a frozen mask, Blaylock swung off his horse. Bogen did likewise. Slocum glanced at the approaching riders; they were still better than halfway across the depression. Ellie nudged her horse and started up to the hilltop.

"No," Slocum said firmly. "You stay down out of sight." Her face darkened with anger. "I need you on one end of the line with that sixteen-shooter of yours. Dane, take that Spencer of yours down to the other end. That way if the jayhawkers try to flank us to get at the herd we'll have more of a chance to stop 'em."

The tension drained from Ellie's face. She nodded, turned the horse, and trotted to the west, then dismounted. "What about you?" Coltrane asked.

"They've seen the three of us," Slocum said. "I propose we go to talk to 'em—if you gentlemen are willing?"

"Count me in," Carrihew said. Velarde just grinned.

With his men—and one woman—belly-down on the

hillside and out of sight, Slocum led his two companions in an easy trot toward the advancing jayhawkers. In a low voice he explained exactly how this hand was to be played. He wasn't thrilled about having to rely on the Mexican, but, damn him, Velarde just listened and nodded as if he were just as aware that Slocum's plans made sense as Lafe Carrihew was.

The five jayhawkers came on at a casual lope. Neither Slocum nor his companions said anything when the two groups reached voice range. They just rode straight, Henry rifles across the pommels of their saddles.

"Howdy, neighbors," called the foremost of the five as he signed his men to a stop ten yards ahead of Slocum. "Fine day, ain't it?"

"Mornin'," Slocum said, reining his own horse in. Velarde and Carrihew halted beside him, precise as a cavalry drill team.

Slocum's drovers were a dusty, raggedy-ass, long-haired group. Up close the jayhawkers made the lot of them look like Silver Kings. Their beards were ragged and spiky, and their hair hung down to their shoulders in greasy strands, or stuck out at odd angles from under the brims of their hats. Two of them wore slouch hats—one, a dark-skinned customer with narrow eyes and a great crow's beak of a nose that Slocum took for some kind of Plains Indian breed, had an eagle feather in the band of his—while another wore a battered plug hat, as well as an eye patch, and the fourth a sweeping sombrero. The man in the center, obviously the leader, wore the oddest hat John Slocum had ever seen, a bizarre and roughly conical fur contraption that towered a good foot above its owner's unshorn head. The men were dressed in clothes as wildly varied as their headgear: frock coats, vests, leather britches, pinstriped trousers, a butternut Confederate dress blouse, and a Yankee sergeant's fatigue jacket, faded almost milky-white at the shoulders. The leader wore a fringed buckskin jacket that hung well past his knees. But more striking than their peculiar garb, more noticeable even than the odor of grease and whiskey and stale sweat that rode the breeze across thirty feet, was their quantity of weapons. The burly, shabby jayhawkers were hung about with an assortment of dirks, hatchets, and Arkansas toothpicks, the leader sported a Sharps carbine decorated along the butt with brass tacks, Indian-fashion, and none sported fewer than three pistols in plain sight. That last fact alone proclaimed them jayhawkers. No honest man had need to go about weighted down under that sort of hardware. In the old days, before revolvers, there were times when prudent men carried three or more pistols with them, since they were good for only one shot apiece. Though the revolver was common by the rise of the border war, it had become a common affectation for ruffians and jayhawkers alike to tote at least three pistols.

The leader squinted his protuberant blue eyes, hawked, and spat. "Slocum! John Slocum! Well, I'm damned."

Slocum was tempted to agree. "Haines."

"Yup. Your old pal and comrade in arms, Sportin' Life Haines. Life's been good to you, Johnny boy." He turned to his comrades and waved an arm expansively, stained buckskin fringe flapping. "This here's my good friend John Slocum. Fought together in the war, we did." He shook his head and piped his eye with a crack-nailed thumb. "To think that fate should cast us ol' comrades together again like this."

"It's shorely a miracle, Sportin' Life," agreed the man in the eye patch and stovepipe hat.

Haines had been a scout for a time attached to the regiment Slocum had served with, in the days before he met Kevin Callahan. The last Slocum had seen of the man was the dun rear end of his horse hurrying in precisely the opposite direction from the Confederate line of advance sometime during the battle of Shiloh. Slocum had been wounded in that battle and spent the better part of a year convalescing. While in hospital he heard that Haines had been exonerated of charges of cowardice on the grounds that a wound had driven his horse into uncontrollable panic. Later, after Slocum had returned to active duty, he heard that Haines and the Army of the Confederacy had parted ways as a result of a misunderstanding concerning a Georgia regiment's payroll that had somehow gone astray shortly after the battle of Chancellorsville.

"What brings you out into the light of day, Sportin' Life?" Slocum asked.

Haines jerked his chin, gesturing past Slocum's shoulder. "Me and the boys understand some Texas yahoos is tryin' to run a herd of diseased cattle through the sovereign state of Kansas. We aim to do our duty and stop 'em. Ain't that so, boys?" The others grinned gap-toothed agreement.

"You can put your mind at ease, Sportin' Life," Slocum said. "That herd's out of New Mexico, not Texas. And those beeves ain't got Texas fever no more'n you do."

The jayhawkers favored Slocum with an appraising squint. "Would you mind tellin' an old army buddy how you come to be privy to that there information?"

"I'm bossin' that drive."

Haines uttered a bark of laughter. The rest of his pack took up the cry. "Well now, it just ain't in me to doubt the word of a old fellow warrior for the Confederacy that he's runnin' a clean herd. Ain't in me a'tall.''

"Tell me one thing, Sportin' Life."

"Anything, Johnny."

"What really happened to that payroll?"

Haines's face sagged into a bloodhound's lugubriousness. "Now, you cain't believe I had anything to do with anything so underhanded nor that, Johnny. You cain't be so cruel."

"Guess not."

"Besides," said Haines with a wink, "them clay-eaters woulda just wasted all that money on booze and whores. Did their souls a service, makin' sure they wasn't set in the way of temptation, an' all." He laughed again, louder than before.

"Been a pleasure talkin' to you, Sportin' Life," Slocum said. "I better be gettin' back to my herd."

"Too bad we gotta get back and let the good folk of Kansas know their cattle're safe," Haines said. "You 'n' me could get together and have us a good hell-raisin', for the sake of old times. Damn shame we cain't do that now."

"Shame," Slocum agreed, and started to turn the paint.

"What're you boys totin' around them damn-Yankee rifles for, boys?" asked the breed in the feathered hat abruptly. "Couldn't be you got a guilty conscience?"

The jayhawkers yipped laughter. "Coyotes, señor," Santiago Velarde said with a flash of white teeth beneath his mustache. "One cannot tell when those varmints will come sneaking around."

The laughter ceased abruptly. Haines turned his men around and took them racing back up the way they'd come. Slocum led the grinning Velarde and the silently watchful Carrihew back toward their own lines at a more stately pace. The muscles of his back tensed in anticipation of the sudden impact of a rifle ball.

The impact didn't come. As they neared the ridge line Slocum saw anxious faces peering over at them. "What happened?" Cookie growled, half in relief and half in disappointment. "They decide not to tangle with us after all?"

Slocum had to smile. "You two help me hold the center of the line," he had time to say to Velarde and Lafe Carrihew.

Then, with a wild cry, a score of jayhawkers poured over the far hill to the attack.

5

Dismounting as he crossed to the south side of the rise, Slocum sent his paint galloping in the direction of the herd with a swat on the rump. Kneeling, he cast an apprehensive glance to his left. Ellie lay on her stomach thirty yards away, peering over a rock at the charging jayhawkers. The hands that gripped her Winchester were white-knuckled with excitement, but otherwise she was outwardly calm as she turned and gave Slocum a quick smile. He felt something tear inside him. *Get back!* he wanted to shout. But he made himself smile back instead.

Holding his Henry in his left hand, he drew his right-hand Colt with his right and gave it a quick check. Since he'd had a St. Louis gunsmith bore through the cylinders of his two Model 1860 Colts and provide them with loading gates he'd been firing the same .44 short rimfire cartridges with them that he did with the Henry. But he still hadn't shaken the reflex of checking to see if the percussion caps were in place before going into action.

A sudden spatter of popping sounds caused several of the drovers to hunch down behind the protective spine of the ridge. "They shoot into the air," Velarde said, peering at the caps set on the nipples of a Dragoon's cylinder. Satisfied, he nodded and slid the weapon back into its holster. "They think to frighten us. We'll show them, ¿qué no?"

The men who'd ducked smiled sheepishly and snugged their weapons against their shoulders. Puffing like a locomotive on a thirty-percent grade, Cookie lumbered up and dropped to the ground beside Slocum. He held a Springfield rifle in both paws and had his huge Sharps pistol stuck in his belt. His apron was stretched taut across his belly like a sail in a stiff breeze.

"Don't shoot before I give the word," Slocum said. With a sneer of derision Bob Ed Bogen raised his rifle. He felt Slocum's needle-sharp gaze and lowered it almost at once, and began probing at his eye with a pale forefinger as if to dislodge a mote of dust.

"Look at them bastards come," Ray Polder muttered.

"But they're bunched together," Velarde said. "Like ducks on a pond, no?"

He was absolutely right. Slocum felt a warm glow inside him. Good old Sportin' Life! Nature had always intended him to be a bandit, not a military man, and for all that he had had a good two years in the regular army he'd managed not to absorb cavalry tactics. If the jayhawkers had spread out into a good wide skirmish line they could have swept past both flanks of the outnumbered defenders and just rolled them up—or gone hell-for-leather for the herd, if they'd preferred. It wouldn't take them an entire minute to scatter a quarter million dollars' worth of steers all over Kansas.

But no, here they came, in a great dirty knot, howling like wolves and wasting powder on the hot blue sky. Two hundred yards, one-fifty, a hundred. Slocum could feel the tension building in the men to either side of him, that strange pre-battle tension that builds in a man's male parts like the itching need to possess a naked, waiting woman. His own tension tied a sour knot in his gut; if somebody triggered off too soon it might startle the jayhawkers into spreading out, and that would mean disaster for the drovers and their hopes of wealth. Remembering his days as a mercenary in Mexico fighting Maximillian, he glanced in Velarde's direction, certain the Mexican would give in first. *The sonofabitch is rolling a cigarette!* he realized.

Fifty yards. Slocum could clearly see Sportin' Life stick a spent revolver in his belt and swing his carbine to his buckskin-clad shoulder. "Now," Slocum said quietly, and squeezed the Henry's trigger.

The ragged volley crashed out to either side of him as Haines's buckskin reared, a dull scarlet patch on its yellow chest. Slocum did feel a certain fondness for an old comrade—hell, Sportin' Life had never stolen any of *his* money, and he'd never much cared for peckerwoods anyway. His next shot took the beak-nosed breed in the throat as the head jayhawker rolled free of his stricken mount.

The drovers prided themselves on their skill with their pistols, but they were lousy shots with a rifle. As Slocum levered his Henry for a third shot he saw one horse go down and another running under an empty saddle. Predictably, all the drovers immediately forgot all their drill in reloading the Springfields. Those with repeaters, however, kept up a cool fire even as their comrades threw down the breechloaders in disgust and clawed leather for the comforting feel of their pistols. From the corner of his eye Slocum saw Velarde pick a howling raider in a Union tunic and knee-high Apache moccasins from the saddle. He fired at a figure indistinct in the thick bank of smoke that hung along the ridge line, missed. Cookie came up to one knee and the Sharps erupted. A sorrel coughed blood and sank to its knees beneath a surprised rider who wore a colorful Hudson's Bay coat in defiance of the heat, twenty feet away. Blaylock shot the man in the belly with one of his Rebel pistols.

Flame stabbed at Slocum and a bullet moaned past his ear. He shoved down the Henry's lever and shouted "Shit!" as it stuck halfway back up. A shell had fed wrong—the gun was useless. And looming over him in the smoke was a one-eyed rider in a tall top hat, his face twisted in a grin of demon triumph as he stared at Slocum down the barrel of a Remington rolling-block pistol. The muzzle yawned wide to swallow Slocum up—

—And the one-eyed man's head exploded in a spray of blood and clotted brains. "I got him!" the wondering Slocum heard Ellie Callahan scream. "I got him!"

Then it was over. Silence fell like the blow of an ax, complete except for the ringing in Slocum's ears from the yammer of the guns. The northerly breeze tore the thick fog of gunsmoke away in wisps to reveal the surviving jayhawkers running away as fast as their wild-eyed foaming horses would carry them. The first of them was just passing Sportin' Life Haines, who was pelting for the far ridge with his buckskin coat hiked up like a frightened milkmaid.

As Slocum's ears cleared he began to hear the screams and groans of the wounded men and horses strewn in front of the ridge line. He heard a drumroll of hooves behind him as he climbed to his feet. He turned and grabbed reflexively at the reins of the tall black horse that tried to surge by, hauling it to a halt by main strength.

"Leave go, damn you!" Cord Blaylock snarled. "We got 'em on the run. Let's chase them coyotes down!"

"No!" Slocum roared. "We can't leave the herd! It's them steers that matters, you crazy sonofabitch!"

Blaylock glared at Slocum with murder in his eyes. "He's right, Cord," Ray Polder said in a soothing voice, rubbing at his chicken neck. "We ran the varmints off. Leave 'em go. They ain't gonna stop this side of the Nebraska line. And we got a drove to get to market."

The Tennessee gunslinger turned his hate-filled eyes on Polder. The older man stood his ground, trailing his Springfield to the earth by the muzzle. Blaylock's reddened eyes swept the group. Then he jerked the reins from Slocum's grip, turned his white-stockinged stud around, and rode back toward the herd, with Bob Ed Bogen trotting at his heels.

Slocum watched him for a minute, then sighed and looked around to take stock of his casualties. He had two. A pistol ball had carried away White Eyes Merriman's right earlobe, which seemed to trouble him not at all. He chatted brightly to Cookie as the burly man patched it with cotton waste and a linen strip. "Just wait'll them *Taoseña* squaws get a load of this," he exclaimed. "They'll just line up to bounce the blankets with old White Eyes!"

The other casualty was Lonesome Dave, who'd had a bullet gouge away a couple of ounces of meat from his left upper arm. He bore his wound with considerably less grace than the older man. "You maggot-ridden sons of army whores!" he roared after the retreating jay-hawkers. "This here shirt was handsewn by a Frog in New Orleans, and you've gone and shot a hole in it!"

Ellie stood over the body of the one-eyed man. She stared with fascination into his face. Her shot had entered his right temple and blown away the left half of his skull, taking with it the eye patch. The good eye that remained stared skyward, startlingly blue. The black-haired woman couldn't seem to take her own eyes from it.

"Ellie?" Slocum stepped forward to grip her arm. It was wire-taut and quivering. "Ellie, are you all right?"

"I shot him," she said, in a high tone he'd never heard from her before. "*I killed him!*" She tittered insanely and suddenly dissolved into tears, dropping her Winchester to cling frantically to Slocum.

He held her close, murmuring what he hoped were encouraging words, stroking her dusty hair. Embarrassed, the men looked in other directions and began drifting off to gather their mounts. The steers were bawling, panic beginning to tinge their voices as the smell of blood and gunsmoke reached them on the heels of the frightening racket of moments before.

Ellie's shivering stopped. After a moment she pulled away. Slocum felt the wet patch on his chest where her tears had soaked through his shirt. The red dust on his shirt had turned to mud around her eyes. She blinked to clear them and brushed a stray strand of hair from her forehead. "I—I'm fine now," she said.

Then she staggered a few steps away and threw up.

It took two hours to get the vast herd into motion again, to start the temperamental longhorns moving—especially after the disturbing sound of gunfire and the dreaded smells of burned powder and spilled blood had brought them dangerously near panic. But the crew Slocum and Callahan had picked for this drove performed beautifully. They were professionals—and the golden vision of Abilene was drawing them on like a magnet.

At Slocum's orders Ellie was placed in the chuck wagon to ride on the stowed bedding until she recuperated. She offered no resistance. He saw her made comfortable, with Cookie hovering and clucking over her like an enormous mother hen, and then went out to see to the field of battle.

A confusion of men and horses lay along the northern slope of the ridge. Six men lay dead; three more moaned and stirred. Slocum nodded with satisfaction at his men's performance. They had inflicted nearly fifty-percent casualties on their foe at the cost of two trifling wounds. Of course Sportin' Life Haines had helped with his foolish head-on charge. Still, the jayhawker wasn't altogether to blame; he'd been counting on panicking the cowboys into flight with his cavalry attack, just as Slocum had counted on routing the sodbusters who'd ambushed the drove a few days before by charging straight into them. But the J-Bar-C drovers had held the line as stoutly as any Johnnies of the Stonewall Brigade could have.

While most of the hands were coaxing the steers into a grudging northward movement, Velarde moved among the injured horses, pausing by each to murmur a few soothing words into the ear of the stricken beast, then blowing out its brains with a 220-grain ball from one of his Dragoons. Then young Doug Travis and his chunky pal Charlie McBride would tie the dead creatures to a harness fixed to a couple of Cookie's mules and drag the bodies away downwind, where their scent could not disturb the skittish steers.

That finished, Velarde walked to where a jayhawker with a gray-streaked brown beard and hair spilling over the shoulders of a black frock coat. The once white linen shirt beneath was a mass of blood and purplish guts: a heavy slug from a Springfield had torn through his belly. "Water," the man groaned. Velarde looked up to Slocum.

Slowly Slocum nodded. Velarde raised the Dragoon and shot the man between his imploring pain-filled eyes.

"You murdering Mexican!" screeched one of the other two wounded, who lay side by side twenty feet along the tawny-grassed slope. As Velarde approached him he tried to scrabble away backwards, kicking with long stork legs and shoving with his one good arm. The shoulder of the other had been turned to mush by another .50-caliber ball. His friend, who had been taken in the upper thigh by a Henry slug, just lay on his side glaring hatred up at Slocum through the layers of dirt, dust, powder smoke, and sweat that masked his bearded features.

"What kind of a white man are you, to let a filthy Meskin murder your own kind?" he spat.

"That Mexican saved your pal a few hours' pain and certain death," Slocum said. "Ain't too many kinds of death worse than a lingering gut wound—burnin's all I can think of." He spat on the ground. "You'd fought a real war instead of ridin' the prairie lookin' for women and kids to cut up and rob, you'd know that. You'd know a sure goner when you see him too."

Unruffled by the conversation, Velarde strolled up to the man with the broken leg and knelt at his side. The man hissed like a treed puma and struck at him clumsily. Without changing expression Velarde clipped him over the ear with the long barrel of his Colt. The man fell back to breathe in bubbling sighs while the Mexican examined his wound. The other jayhawker proved more sensible; he contented himself with glaring ferociously at Velarde when it came his turn to be looked over.

Doug and Charlie had set about removing the dead men from the drove's path. Both looked a little green around the gills. "With care these two could recover, señor," Velarde called to Slocum from beside the jayhawkers. "What shall we do with them?"

Slocum had his mind made up already. "Charlie, Doug, you finish with them stiffs, and then move these gentlemen off to the side too. They can have the honor o' standin' honor guard for their fallen comrades."

The two jayhawkers burst into frantic protest. Slocum turned away.

The white-hot disc of the sun was well past the zenith when the bawling, reluctant herd crossed the ridge that had been the scene of a battle a few short hours before. "Move 'em out!" John Slocum shouted to his men. "We got Abilene waitin' for us, and we gotta get there first to get the gold."

"No!" screamed the skinny jayhawker with the busted shoulder. "No, you cain't just leave us here like this! It ain't hooman!"

Slocum turned his pony's nose and trotted across the front of the herd. He halted the animal in front of where the two men lay. A buzzing black cloud of flies seethed on the bodies of horses and men nearby. The stink was getting on intolerable.

Slocum unclipped a canteen from his belt and threw it to the man with the hole in his leg. "There now. That oughta keep you boys for a day or so—even in this sun."

The men's faces were stark, taut and white as an artist's stretched canvas. The skinny one licked cracked, swollen lips. "But what if nobody finds us?"

Slocum shook his head. "Surely you fellers don't think your pals would up and abandon you, do you?" Their faces gave eloquent reply. Laughing, he turned the paint and loped back to his place at the front of the moving mass of cattle.

"Wait!" the two marauders screeched in a frantic cawing chorus. "Don't leave us! We'll die sure!"

Each of Slocum's drovers looked at the helpless, hopeless pair as they went past, keeping that great herd in motion. Some looked contemptuous, some impassive, and one or two paused, as if about to protest abandoning the wounded men here to almost certain death by exposure. And one by one the drovers turned their faces forward again, to the vision of Abilene and wealth lying beyond the northeastern horizon, and rode unheeding on.

6

"A word with you, Slocum." The daydream image of stacks of gold bars gleaming in the hot Kansas sun vanished. Slocum blinked and halfturned in the saddle.

"What's on your mind, White Eyes?" he asked.

The older man raised his hat and wiped sweat off his forehead. A red smear of mud came away with his hand. His red and white flannel shirt was soaked with big half-moons of sweat under his armpits, and his chestnut mare's flanks glistened with the moisture of heat and exertion. The stocky, sandy-haired wrangler had been riding herd on the drove's remuda. A quick glance told Slocum that Merriman had called young Mc-Bride over to spell him while he talked to the boss.

The older man settled his Spencer carbine across his pommel. "You know I been a freighter sometimes, down in the southern part of New Mexico Territory and over to Arizona," he said. "Apache country. Spend enough time down there and you start to get a feel for certain things, 'less you get dead." He looked sidelong at Slocum with his water-pale eyes. "We bein' followed."

"Know that."

Merriman chuckled. "Figgered you would. What do we do about it?"

The paint bobbed its head and whuffled irritation. It

was too hot for a horse to work, and the beast wondered why Slocum didn't have sense enough to see that plain fact.

Casual-seeming, Slocum raised his head and scanned the horizon. The herd had come into another area of gently rising and falling land. To an eye used to the ruggedness of New Mexico, the land seemed board-flat, and mostly was. But here that appearance was deceiving. At the moment the steers were trudging their way through a vast, shallow bowl. It would be no trick for a few alert horsemen to observe the unwieldy mob of cattle without letting themselves be seen.

"Drop back and pass the word. Don't make no big deal over it. Just have the boys here on the left flank put a little more distance between themselves and the herd, and tell 'em to keep a sharp lookout."

Merriman nodded and let his horse drop back. In a few moments he was riding knee-to-knee with Lafe Carrihew, who was holding swing a couple of hundred yards behind Slocum. Slocum urged his horse into a lazy trot and forged out in front of the lead steers. Having been on the move from sunup to midmorning, the herd was strung out into a long, attenuated arrowhead, broad behind, narrowing to a point in front. Across the tip of the arrow from Slocum rode Velarde, who today was wearing a black vest embroidered with silver thread, and beneath it a bleached linen shirt that fairly gleamed in the bright sunlight.

"You've noticed we're being shadowed, señor," the Mexican greeted him.

Swallowing a surge of irritation, Slocum nodded. He gave Velarde the same set of instructions he'd given Merriman, to alert the men on the right flank. The Mexican fell back to spread the alert, and Slocum took up his post on right point.

In a few moments Slocum heard a flurry of hoofbeats and up rode Ellie, her cheeks flushed with excitement. "What is it?" she demanded. "More sodbusters?"

He frowned. In the three days since the battle with the jayhawkers they'd had four run-ins with sodbusters trying to turn them back. Two of them had been deputations, one of four frightened men on horseback who had accepted Slocum's assurances that his herd was clean and his men of peaceable intent with obvious relief, the other of a dozen men on foot armed with clubs, pitchforks, and a couple of shotguns with their foregrips wired to their rusty barrels, and one old muzzle-loading Springfield rifled musket. This group exuded belligerence and a pronounced aroma of whiskey. The alert, hard-faced, well-armed appearance of Slocum's band took the steam out of them; these were no bored cowboys slouching along and marking time until they delivered their charges to market. Slocum's men had the drive and determination of fanatics. Wealth was waiting for them, not the few bucks' payoff a common dusty-ass wrangler could look forward to, but *money*. With that promise before them, and John Slocum to lead them to it, they were damned if they'd let anything stand in their way—least of all a passel of half-assed farmers with sticks and blunderbusses. After a good hard look at Slocum and company they were only too glad to stand aside—but only after they'd told Slocum what had brought them out to contest the herd's right-of-way. Like the more pacific contingent the day before, they had recently been visited by another herd bound for Abilene, and that one's passage had left few friends behind.

Slocum's drive was gaining on Billy Lancer's.

The third encounter with angry farmers had been potentially the worst of the lot. Slocum knew full well that

the high-strung, stampede-prone steers were the real
weakness of the drove, not the men who guarded them.
Lined out along hundreds of yards of prairie, the herd
presented a long, vulnerable flank. Early in the morning
of the day before, a party of men on horseback had
come booming over a rise and ridden straight down on
the left flank of the herd, shooting, hollering, and waving their hats in the air—obviously trying to spook the
steers. Knowing the danger as well as Slocum did, the
drovers reacted quickly. Lafe Carrihew had emptied the
sixteen rounds from his Henry at the attackers in what
sounded like one continuous report. He only winged
one of the charging farmers, but his barrage had the
desired effect. The attack faltered, and then White Eyes
opened with his Spencer and Cord Blaylock clipped
another of the riders with a lucky shot from his sixguns.
Slocum and the rest had had their hands full trying to
keep the steers from fleeing the sound of gunfire;
Slocum had also been too busy to prevent Ellie riding
around the rear of the herd to fling a few shots at the
retreating men from her Winchester.

The sudden assault had disrupted the herd enough so
that it took an hour to get all the steers going the right
way again—which was little enough, considering the
catastrophe that might have occurred. But then, as the
sun dipped toward the featureless western horizon and
the daylight started washing out to gray and blue,
Lonesome Dave Shapp, whose eyes were as sharp as his
taste in clothes, spotted riders lurking in a stand of cottonwood trees on the near side of a stream that lay in the
drove's path. Ellie was riding point, and her blood was
up from the morning's action. With a wild yell she
charged, yanking the Winchester out and blazing away
as she rode. Her flat Andalusian hat came off and her
black hair streamed like a wild banner behind her.

Slocum and a handful of the others had been forced to follow as best they could, Slocum cursing with every beat of his pony's unshod feet.

The sight of the black-haired Fury bearing down on them like vengeance on horseback unnerved the would-be ambushers—if that's what they were—and they fled across the stream and disappeared without firing a shot. Ellie had reined her chestnut to a rearing halt among the trees, shaken her rifle derisively at the backs of the retreating riders, and trotted back to meet Slocum with her cheeks flushed and her eyes burning like beacons.

He'd recognized the look. She'd had it that night after she killed Sportin' Life Haines's one-eyed lieutenant, when they were alone and Slocum explained to her that most men reacted the same way she had to killing their first man, and that she had nothing to be ashamed of. She'd gotten that look then, and practically eaten Slocum alive. The look made his crotch crawl with desire for her, but he'd lit into her all the same, stripping the hide off her for putting herself in danger.

She was too proud or too smart to argue with him in front of the men. Besides, this time he was right, and they both knew it; she'd taken a foolish risk. So she had sat in her saddle and taken her tongue-lashing without reply.

And last night had been a lonely one for John Slocum. From the slow burn Ellie seemed to do every time he got near her, tonight was shaping up the same.

Something of that mad light was burning in her green eyes now. "Don't know," Slocum told her. "I don't think it's the farmers this time."

A shout from the herd's left flank brought their heads around. Ellie drew in her breath sharply.

Four riders had appeared on the high ground to the northwest, silhouetted against a sky streaked with mare's tails of white cloud. For a moment they sat, un-moving as statues, gazing down upon the bawling herd. Then they turned and were gone.

Slocum let out a long breath he didn't know he'd been holding. "We got trouble."

"What do you mean?" Ellie asked.

"You see that rider in the middle, big hombre with a derby hat on?" She nodded. "That's John Burnham. An Englishman, they call him the Duke." Slocum's lip curled. "He's Billy Lancer's sidekick. Been with him since his days with Quantrill."

Ellie's mouth tightened to a line. "Do you know who that was, Slocum?" a voice demanded from behind.

Cord Blaylock was loping up on his flashy black, with Bob Ed as always coming right behind. "Those were Lancer's men!" the Tennessean said.

"That's right," Slocum replied evenly.

Blaylock looked at him hard. "Well? Aren't you going to do something about it?"

"About what?"

Bob Ed hooted. "Lissen at him, Cord. The durn fool don't even know what you're talkin' about!"

"Billy Lancer's men are following us, Slocum. Don't you intend to do something about it?"

"What would you suggest I do?"

"Why, chase them down. Teach 'em a real lesson." He smiled unpleasantly. "I'll be glad to lead a pursuit party, if you'd prefer to stay with the herd."

"Why, that's right big of you, Cord. You're offerin' to go harin' off chasing shadows. Be real handy if Lancer's men come boomin' down on the herd and find just a skeleton crew to guard it. He couldn't ask for a better opportunity, now, could he?"

The big man turned red and a vein pulsed in his fore-head. "You're pushing your luck, Slocum."

"Damn straight. I'm pushing my luck clear to Abilene, Kansas, and Joe Callahan's herd along with it. And I ain't gonna get drawn into any wild goose chases while I'm doin' it."

Dane Andersen and Ray Polder were coming up along the right side of the drove. "What're we gonna do, Johnny?"

"Keep our eyes open and our powder dry."

Blaylock looked from the two men to Slocum. "It could be that what this drove needs is a little change of management," he said softly.

At this Ellie flared like powder in a pan. "My father put John Slocum in charge of this drive, Cord Blaylock. And he'll stay in charge until these beeves reach Abilene!"

A slow smile spread across Blaylock's lean face. "If *you* say so, little lady," he said, and rode back to his position. Bob Ed Bogen flipped Slocum a sneer and followed. A moment later Andersen and Polder exchanged glances and turned away too.

Slocum reached into his pocket and pulled out a bag of Bull Durham. "I'm gonna have to shoot that man," he said matter-of-factly, dallying the reins around his saddle horn and shaking some tobacco onto a paper. As he deftly rolled a cigarette he looked up at the horizon, where clouds were beginning to pile higher and higher. "Unless Billy Lancer does it for me."

The clouds that had been scattered across the sky congealed into a swollen mass as morning turned into afternoon. Slocum and the men divided their tension between the herd, the horizon, and the increasingly threatening sky. Several times that afternoon a cry from a sharp-eyed wrangler brought heads snapping around to see riders on the skyline, loping along parallel to the herd or just sitting and watching. It was all too apparent that they were letting themselves be seen, now and again, to keep the drovers on edge. It was devilishly effective. Long before sundown, when a lid of leaden cloud lay between the flat prairie and the sun, the men of the J-Bar-C rode fingering their weapons and swinging their eyes from side to side, drawn wire-taut with expectation of imminent attack.

Worst of all from Slocum's viewpoint was that it was Ellie Callahan's turn to ride lead. She had Lonesome Dave with her, which set Slocum's mind somewhat at ease. For all his fancy habits of dress—and his bandaged arm—he was a steady man, and he had the eyes of a cat. They were often turned Miss Ellie's way, which didn't particularly bother Slocum. Elianora Callahan had made it abundantly clear where her attentions lay.

But Slocum's heart jumped into his mouth when, not ten seconds after the two lead riders vanished over a rise ahead, Lonesome Dave reappeared, riding flat out toward the herd.

The sound of weapons being cocked crackled down both sides of the drove as the wranglers prepared for the arrival of the long-awaited attack. As if to echo the ripple of metallic sound a boom of distant thunder rolled overhead, drawing nervous high-pitched cries from the herd. "If Lancer's men come now, so much the better for us, no?" Velarde called across the backs of the lead animals. "If a thunderstorm hits his herd when his men are attacking us, I don't think he'll have so much to show even if he reaches Abilene." The Mexican's voice was airy and unconcerned. Slocum opened his mouth to curse the man for joking at a time like this, and then shut it with a click. Despite the grin frozen into place beneath the crow's-wing sweep of his mustache, Velarde was watching the place Ellie had disappeared with every bit of concern as was John Slocum.

Shapp had passed the chuck wagon now. Cookie's bullwhip cracked like a pistol above the backs of his mules as he urged the team forward, as though he meant to take the wagon lumbering to Ellie's aid. Unable to contain himself, Slocum loped his horse forward to meet the gunslinger.

"There's a rider comin'," Shapp shouted.

"What in Christ's name did you leave Miss Ellie alone for?"

Shapp laughed. He had a high-pitched laugh for a man. "You should know by now how much good it does to argue with that lady."

Slocum scowled and goaded the little paint with his broad spurs. As Shapp turned his mount around, Velarde joined them at a gallop. His handsome face was stiff.

The first thing that caught John Slocum's eye as they topped the rise was the glint of sunlight off the steep shake roofs of a small town a mile or two ahead. A shaft of slanting afternoon light had broken through the clouds to reflect off buildings made shiny by a brief shower. Considerably closer was the moving speck of a lone rider, black against the gray land.

Ellie was waiting with one hand on her hip and her head held high. She didn't turn as Slocum and the others thudded up alongside. "What do you make of it?" Slocum asked her.

"I don't know," she answered. "I don't think it's threatening, whatever it is."

Off to the left, yellow-white lightning stabbed the horizon. "Dave, get back and tell the boys to stop the herd. Don't want to try runnin' those beeves by a town this late. An' it'd be good to have the steers settled in for the night before the storm breaks." Shapp rode off, leaving the three to await the single horseman.

As he drew close enough for them to make out details, it seemed that Ellie was right in her estimation. The rider was a portly little man with a full-moon face and a ridiculous plug hat, at least two sizes too small, perched atop his head. He wore a frock coat, white shirt with celluloid collar, and a blue string tie that seemed to glow even in the diffuse light. His "horse" was an astonishing blue-eyed pinto mule with a bite taken out of one ear.

"Howdy," he called, as the mule puffed up the slope toward the trio. "Name's Hobart. I'm the mayor of McMurtyville, and I have the extreme pleasure of welcoming you to our little community."

Ellie looked at Slocum in amazement. He gave her a slight shrug. This made no more sense to him than to her.

"I'm John Slocum," he said. "This here's Miss Elianora Callahan, of the J-Bar-C Ranch, New Mexico Territory. Her daddy owns the herd we're drivin' to Abilene."

"I'm pleased to meet you, your honor," she said, smiling.

He swept his hat from his head and bowed from the saddle. The buttons of his shirt threatened to pop from the strain his amply belly put on them. "I'm overwhelmed by the honor of meeting you, ma'am. And you, Mr. Slocum, and you, Mr.—?" He looked expectantly at Velarde, whom Slocum had neglected to introduce.

"Santiago Velarde, *a sus órdenes*."

"Pleasure to meet you, sir. Pleasure." He righted himself with a grunt of effort. "Well, sirs and mademoiselle, I've come to offer you the hospitality of our town. We're holding a little fandango in honor of your arrival, tonight at the town hall. We'd be purely honored to have you and your men attend.''

Fighting the inclination of his jaw to sag in amazement, Slocum said, ''But how did you know we were coming?''

Mayor Hobart beamed all over his pie-pan face. ''Why, your good friend Mr. William Lancer told us so.''

7

The inside of the town hall was a blaze of yellow light. A table occupied one of the long walls of the high-raftered room. It sported a shiny red and white oilcloth cover and fairly groaned under the weight of hams, roasts of beef, several roasted chickens, baskets of steaming hot rolls, and ears of white corn. A vast earthenware bowl was heaped high with mashed potatoes, and its twin sat nearby, wreathed in steam rising from hot brown gravy. Whiskey bottles in orderly ranks stood guard over the fantastic feast.

"*Madre de Dios*," Velarde breathed.

"They really laid it on for us, didn't they?" said Lonesome Dave Shapp, smoothing his freshly waxed mustache and swelling his chest with a deep breath. " 'Course they'll more'n make their roll back from the supplies Cookie's buyin'." He shook his head. "Dunno how much I care for hospitality that's bought and sold."

"You'd rather they were shooting at us, señor?"

"I guess I wouldn't, Santiago."

Slocum allowed himself a smile and sipped whiskey from a glass. Maybe the people of McMurtyville wouldn't be as openly friendly to the drovers if they didn't think they'd turn a profit on the deal. But that didn't make Slocum much never-mind. Before he'd set Cookie loose at the general store he'd looked over prices and found them reasonable enough. Since the Texas-fever scare had mostly dried up the cattle drives running this way since midsummer, McMurtyville could definitely use the J-Bar-C wranglers' custom. Their pleasure at seeing them was quite genuine.

And besides, as Velarde said, it was better than having them shoot at the drovers.

He sipped again. Lonesome Dave was talking through his fancy bell-crown hat anyway. No drover on the trail ever got hospitality that wasn't bought and paid for, and usually at far more outrageous prices than the citizens of McMurtyville seemed to expect.

But there were still a lot of unanswered questions in John Slocum's mind. Billy Lancer figured prominently in all of them. While they remained to be answered, he took comfort from the weight of the rebored Colts on his hips, and from the presence of Lonesome Dave at his side. And, grudgingly, from Velarde's presence too.

"My, what handsome men!" The cooing voice belonged to Mayor Hobart's pouter pigeon of a wife, Emmeline, a plump and pleasant, if somewhat cross-eyed, woman with blond hair piled high atop her head. "I simply can't tell you how happy we all are to have you in our town!"

Velarde caught up her hand and pressed it to his lips. "It could not be as happy as we are to be here." She blushed clear from her cheeks to the not inconsiderable expanse of cleavage exposed by her blue dress. Apparently she'd put on her city-bought best for the occasion.

"Why, aren't you gallant, sir," she fluttered. "You're just as gallant a gentleman as that Mr. Lancer, and that's saying some."

For all his suavity, Santiago Velarde goggled a little at that. "Beggin' your pardon, ma'am," Slocum said, "but now that you mention—"

"Well I'll be damned," breathed Lonesome Dave Shapp.

Throughout the packed hall heads swiveled to the door. The wheezy little five-piece band tooting and thumping away up on the raised dais at the far end of the chamber missed a beat. John Slocum felt his heart do the same.

Ellie Callahan had entered. She wore a dress some friendly local woman had lent her. It was a confection of green silk, a silk that matched the emerald of her eyes and perfectly complemented her sun-darkened skin and raven-black hair. It was an off-the-shoulder design, with a daring neckline and a big bow in the back. As Mrs. Hobart, who fortunately seemed to have missed Dave Shapp's bit of self-appraisal, bustled off amiably to take the newcomer under her wing, John Slocum knew he'd never seen a more beautiful woman in his life.

Somehow he found the realization unnerving.

She walked across the scuffed hardwood floor, and all eyes followed her. "You like it, John?" she asked, a shy hesitation in her voice.

"It's beautiful," he said from a throat abruptly gone dust-dry.

She came to him. Some instinct made him hold out his arm, and she slipped her arm around it. Lonesome Dave tipped his hat to her and allowed himself to be escorted off toward the food table by a handsome matron with a touch of gray in the hair drawn up in a bun at the back of her neck, and a look in her eye which, coupled with the way she swung her hips as they walked together, told Slocum Lonesome Dave wasn't liable to be coming back to the drove before dawn. A pair of giggling blond girls with their hair in ponytails captured Velarde. The way the bodices of their demure frocks pushed out in front, they probably weren't as young as they appeared at first glance. And there wasn't anything at all little-girlish about the way they eyed the whip-slim Mexican in his elegant, tight-cut clothes. Mexicans were generally despised in Texas and New Mexico, but up here it seemed they were something of a novelty.

"Looks as if Santiago's struck it lucky," Ellie said. Slocum grunted noncommittally.

They made their way to the table across the crowded floor. Ellie was as elegant as some European countess, smiling and nodding graciously to the townspeople who greeted them. Slocum didn't have to say a word, just nod his head from time to time in reasonably courteous fashion. He was uncomfortable in crowds, uncomfortable in social settings of this stripe. He sensed that Ellie knew this and was compensating for him, and that made him uneasy too. Did she know him too well?

"Did you find out about that Lancer person?" she asked as they stood eating from earthenware plates. "Everyone I heard talked about him as if he were a combination of General Lee, Leonardo da Vinci, and the Duke of Buckingham."

Having heard of only the first-named of those individuals, Slocum shrugged. "Ain't had much of a chance," he said, tearing into a chicken wing with his strong white teeth. "All's I can say is he must be on his best behavior—an' he must have a reason."

"Certainly the way these people talk about him is different from everything I've heard before. It's as if they're talking about two different people."

•   •   •

"Lancer's smart, and slippery as a snake. He can put on a real good act when he wants to." Slocum took a quick gulp of whiskey. A fresh gout of rain hit the sloped tin roof of the town hall like a charge of buckshot. Slocum thought of the men back at the camp. This was a miserable night to be a drover. Rain made the steers uneasy, like just about everything else, but at least there hadn't been much thunder. That was what really spooked them. However, it wouldn't be too long before Slocum was back out on the range in a yellow slicker baby-sitting the cows. That was the arrangement they'd worked out: He'd split the party up into several groups, so that one could come into town while the others stood watch, and then rotate so that everybody got to sample McMurtyville's unexpected hospitality. Lonesome Dave and even Velarde might be slightly delayed when their turn to go back came, but Ellie would insist on returning on time. She was like that.

He looked past her at a sudden commotion at the doorway to the hall. "John—your face," she exclaimed. "Why are you looking that way?" Then her eyes followed his to see what had turned his features to a grim, stark mask—one she had never seen, even in the heat of battle.

Two men had stepped into the hall and placed themselves on either side of the portal as if they were guarding it. One she didn't know, a slender man in black with a gambler's narrow good looks and slicked-back hair, but the other she had seen. He was a huge man with an enormous red-bay mustache and a round derby hat, which he doffed to reveal a smooth and hairless dome of a skull. A blocky shelf of brow overhung a nose that had been broken so many times as to be virtually shapeless. The eyes that looked out of that brutal face were green, glittering with an unlooked-for intelligence.

Another man swept through the door like an actor coming on stage and stopped. He did not speak or make any display, simply stood—but all eyes turned toward him. He was a tall man, almost as tall as John Slocum. He was dressed in a white linen shirt, brown leather vest open in front, and brown trousers. He was bareheaded. Two pistols rode in tooled-leather holsters at his waist, and there his gunbelt was designed in a way unfamiliar to Ellie, with loops sewn into it to hold shiny brass cartridges.

At first glance she didn't think he was a particularly handsome man. He had a boyish look to him, almost cherubic, with open features and a halo of curly yellow hair surrounding them. It was only when his blue eyes found hers and he smiled that she felt the full force of his presence.

John Slocum spat a single word: "*Lancer.*"

Plump little Mayor Hobart and his plump little wife chugged up to greet the newcomers with cries of delight. Lancer smiled gratefully, apparently shy at being fussed over, as the mayor pumped his hand. Then Hobart puffed up to the dais at the other end of the hall and clambered up in front of the band, while his wife stood by Billy Lancer, gazing up at him as though he'd just ridden down from heaven on a golden cloud.

"Ahem!" Mayor Hobart harrumphed for attention. Conversation died and the band came to a stop with a final plunking of untuned piano keys. "Ladies and gentlemen of McMurtyville, we are today honored to have amongst us a number of prominent cattlemen—and one lovely cattlewoman, if I, er, may coin a phrase." Polite applause. Mrs. Hobart clapped more enthusiastically than all the others put together. *I can see why he married her*, John Slocum thought.

"First, we have three gentlemen who have been our

guests for two days, and may already be familiar to you: Mr. William Lancer, bossing the Lazy Lightning drive from the great and sovereign state of Texas"—here there were a few sour looks from Union army vets at the use of the word "sovereign"—"and his esteemed associates, Mr. John Burnham and Mr. James Sinclair." Much more vigorous applause, much of it by young—and not so young—ladies looking at Billy Lancer with some fixedness.

Hobart turned. "And over here, our newly arrived but equally honored guests, Mr. John Slocum, who is heading the drove from the J-Bar-C Ranch in New Mexico Territory, and his companions, Mr. David Shapp and See-nyor Santiago Velarde." More applause, and Slocum wasn't too displeased to see that some of the ladies seemed to be showing a more than merely polite interest in him.

"And finally," Hobart said, swelling his chest like a male sand grouse in a mating dance, "we are most especially honored by the lovely presence of Miss Elianora Callahan, daughter of the owner of the J-Bar-C, who is accompanying her father's herd." This time it was the men who stared and clapped to beat the band, with no little bugging of eyes and the occasional wolf-whistle from the younger gentry.

"So let's make them all feel at home!" Hobart concluded. The weedy oldster who played the trumpet produced a fanfare that put Slocum in mind of a brass statue farting, and Hobart hopped down from the stage as the band lurched into a lively galop.

Slocum tensed as the mayor approached with Billy Lancer in tow. It took all his willpower to keep his face impassive and his hand away from his Colt. Ellie gave his arm a surreptitious squeeze of encouragement.

When they were but a few paces away Lancer stepped

forward, thrusting out his hand. "John Slocum! It's good to see you. It's been a long time." John could feel surprise emanating from Ellie. He saw little choice but to stick out his hand and shake with Lancer, muttering some greeting of his own.

Looking a little put out at having his thunder stolen, Hobart said, "It appears you two gentlemen are acquainted."

"Oh, indeed," Lancer said. "Mr. Slocum and I are old friends. We were once comrades in arms together—on the other side, I suspect, from most of the noble gentlemen of your town, but what's done is done. Isn't that right?" He said the last as if Mayor Hobart's agreement mattered as much to him as drawing his next breath; mollified and flattered, the mayor bobbed his head and said, yes, yes, that was right as rain.

Lancer turned to Ellie. "And you, lovely lady—I can't tell you how pleased I am to meet you." She extended her hand. He raised it to his lips and kissed it. His eyes met hers over their clasped hands, and a red flush spread from her cheeks down her graceful neck.

"You're a wonder," he said, keeping hold of her hand. "To be able to ride in the dust of your drove all day, and yet at night unfold so trim and beautiful and fresh as a primrose blossom."

It was flattery of the rawest sort. Slocum was not pleased to see that none of it seemed to be sticking in Ellie's throat. "You are too kind, sir," she said, a touch breathlessly.

"By no means. I can't be too kind to the daughter of Joseph Callahan—or the sister of Lieutenant Kevin Callahan, CSA."

Her eyes widened in confusion and surprise. "Yes, I know your brother's name, dear lady. It burns brightly in the heart of any true son of the Confederacy—

meaning no disrespect, your honor." His other hand rose to join the right in clasping Ellie's fervently. "The glory your brother earned at Gettysburg would be famed as far as that of the Yankee Cushing, had things turned out differently. But those who knew him cherish the memory within our hearts."

By this time Ellie looked as if she were about to melt into a pool on the floor. "The Duke spotted you on the trail today when he and some of the boys were out rounding up some strays," Lancer said to Slocum. He shook his head. "We've had a rough time of it. I hope you've fared better, old friend."

"Mr. Lancer tells us the jayhawkers are thick as flies down south of here," Mrs. Hobart said in tones of delicious horror.

I could tell you a few things about Mr. Lancer. "We had a little trouble," Slocum said. "Nothin' serious."

Lancer grinned as if that were the best news he'd heard since rising. "Good to hear it. Ah, but I perceive the band is commencing a favored Strauss waltz. Will you do me the honor?" And he swept Ellie out onto the floor to join the dancing couples. He'd never once relinquished her hand.

"Isn't he a remarkable man?" burbled Mrs. Hobart.

"He ain't kidding his boys have had it rough," the mayor said. "Rode in without so much as a moldy coffee bean by way of supplies. Jayhawkers burned their commissary wagon, down by Rawson. Mr. Lancer's men were lucky to get away with their herd and their lives."

So the sodbusters had scored one on Lancer. Good for them. Slocum couldn't entirely keep down a grin of satisfaction.

But looking out at the dance floor it was easy enough to twist the smile to a grimace. John Slocum had the musical sensibilities of a creosoted railroad tie, and when he danced did so with the easy grace of a man with one foot trapped in a spittoon. Lancer slid Ellie through the swirling couples like an otter through water. Her face was that of someone in a dream, and none too eager to awaken.

"Señor Slocum." He shook himself and looked around to see Velarde standing at his side. The Mexican smiled and nodded his head in the direction of the buffet. The blond sisters were casting coy glances their way and giggling. "I wondered if I might stay a little longer than I planned. Dane Anderson said I could take his turn in town if I wanted. He's a family man, you know."

"Velarde," Slocum rasped, "I don't give a damn if you never come back." And he walked off to pour himself another whiskey.

Maybe two.

Rain hammered with a hundred million tiny fists on the arched canopy of the Studebaker supply wagon. Wearied and wet to the bone by four hours' watch over the herd, John Slocum and Ellie clambered stiffly over the tailgate and began to struggle out of their dripping rain slickers. The oiled-cloth coats steamed in the yellow glow of a single lantern, and the humid cavern of the wagon was thick with the aroma of coffee beans, gunpowder, soaked wood, and canvas.

After returning from town to spend a grueling four hours tending to the steers, John Slocum wanted nothing more than to close his eyes and let himself drop into the abyss of unconsciousness on whose edge he'd been teetering for what seemed a lifetime. Even though this storm was thankfully attended by little lightning, the rain and cold made the longhorns uneasy and irritable, unable to rest. They tended either to wander off into the night and have to be urged back to the drove with a tact usually reserved for guiding visiting dignitaries through battle zones, or blunder into one another and begin to paw raw gouges in the wet red earth and bellow indignant challenges, threatening riot. With horses and riders no more happy or comfortable than their charges, and the mud often as slippery as oil under foot and hoof, endurance of man—or woman—and animal was tested to the utmost.

Pallets had been arranged in the front of the wagon. Slocum's eyes shut the instant his head touched the rolled-up bedroll that served as a pillow. But sleep was to be denied him for a while yet.

He felt warm lips on his mouth, a strong, insistent tongue probing between his teeth. He responded unconsciously, all but unwillingly, reaching up as if to fend off the amorous assault.

His hands touched bare flesh, chill and seal-slick with dampness. His eyes flew open. Ellie lay atop him, her sodden flannel shirt discarded on a pile of flour sacks, her heavy bare breasts pressed against his chest.

Instantly the weight of exhaustion fell away from him. He kneaded the succulent flesh of her breasts as her fingers tugged at his belt, stiff and swollen with the rain. Her nipples were as hard and cool as smooth-washed pebbles in a streambed against his palms.

At last his waterlogged britches were opened. Her fingers massaged him to a throbbing frenzy as she fumbled with her own garment. He stirred, half rising and turning to her, unbuttoning the fly of her jeans and skinning them from her slender hips with a convulsive heave. He thrust a hand roughly between her legs as she battled the recalcitrant pants down her thighs, feeling the crispness of her so-neat triangle of midnight-colored hair, and the satiny softness and moistness that waited within. Finally one slim leg wrenched free of the encumbering pants leg. With a cry of triumph and passion Slocum thrust forward, entering her full-length at a stroke, pinning her hard rump against the wall of the wagon. She gasped and called his name and grabbed tufts of his hair as if to pull it out by the roots as he withdrew and slammed himself home again. Her hips met his, grinding in animal abandon as her own passion mounted uncontrollably.

It wasn't making love; that was too polite a name for it, too refined. It had something of the heedless mating of healthy animals, wild and free, in it, and something of sadism, too, of Slocum taking vengeance for the attention Ellie had shown his hated rival, Lancer. But as he took the black-haired beauty in the yellow murk of that dank canvas cavern, he sensed a dark requital in the wanton, hungering movements of her lithe body, a need beyond lust, as if she sought to slake anger, resentment, or frustration in this coupling.

With a panther's cry Slocum spent himself in a driving fury that slammed Ellie's tailbone against the wagon's side again and again in staccato rhythm, and with a panther's cry she answered him. Her whole pale body tensed like wound wire, clamping him with every fine-drawn muscle in a shuddering spasm of repletion. Then the breath sighed out of her, and she melted against him, warm and pliable as melting butter.

"We need to find a better place for this," she breathed. "I think my tail's rubbed raw. Also I've picked up a few splinters in unfortunate places."

Embarrassed to hear her talking like this—she was a fine lady, after all, not some cheap saloon girl who sold love by the minute—Slocum muttered some apology.

She laughed, low and husky and deep in her throat. "Don't apologize, silly boy."

They lay together listening to the rain. Slocum took animal pleasure in stroking her naked squeaky-moist skin, the ripe full feel of her snuggled against his hard-muscled body. *A man could come to like this*, he told himself.

"That Billy Lancer's quite a charming young man," Ellie said. Slocum stiffened slightly. "It's hard to believe he's as wicked as they say."

"Back during the war, he had a favorite little trick for questioning captives," Slocum rasped. "Used to take a Yankee soldier didn't want to answer questions, smear his feet with pitch, and set 'em off. Used to brag he could git answers out of a bronze statue of Winfield Scott that way."

A lesser woman might have gone into hysterics at the brutal story. Ellie shuddered once and hugged Slocum more tightly. "Do you think he'll try to do something to stop us?" she asked.

"Dunno. Ain't much he can do, just now. He's already lost time from stirrin' up trouble with folks as he passed through. I don't think even he dares rile up these McMurtyville folks by hittin' us, not when he's camped just the other side of Sawyer's Creek, there north of town. If our boys and a posse from McMurtyville set out after him, there ain't no way he'd get clear, slowed down by his herd." For a moment he lay stroking Ellie's rain-lank hair. "Still, 'tain't like him to have us this near to hand and not do nothin' about it."

Ellie rolled to her side and looked at him with her green eyes glowing in the lantern light. "You were awfully rough on Santiago," she said. "What have you got against him?"

Slocum set his jaw. "He's a Mexican."

"What has that got to do with anything? He's worked for Dad for years, and Dad says no better man's ever sat saddle leather."

Slocum sighed and rolled onto his back. Overhead the canvas canopy was bowed by the weight of gathering water, beginning to stain as wetness seeped through. *Have to move the blankets when that starts to drip,* he thought.

"Back in '65, when the war ended and it looked like mebbe the Yankees was gonna start stringin' up ever'body who'd wore the butternut, a bunch of us soldiers signed up with ol' General Selby to go fight for Juarez against the Frenchies, down in Mexico. Promised gold and land, and that looked pretty good to men without no money nor homes and mebbe nothin' to look forward to but the noose.

"So we went down, and fought the French, and whipped 'em when we met them. I found me a girl, lovely little thing. Named Consuelo. Eyes just like a fawn, hair long and black and glossy-like, like yours." For a moment he lay silent, fingers laced behind his head, staring with unfocused eyes at the sagging wagon top. "Some no-good sonofabitch informed, told the Frenchies she was a spy. A patrol went out to her village—this was after us mercenaries had pulled up stakes and moved on—and they arrested her. Gave her three minutes to confess to a priest, then stood her against the wall of the church and shot her. She weren't more than seventeen."

"That's terrible," Ellie said.

"Since then," Slocum said, "never have had much use for Mexicans. *Or* Frenchmen."

Ellie lay watching him for a handful of heartbeats. Then: "What're you going to do, John? After this is over, and you have your money?"

"Ain't rightly thought about it," he lied.

Her fingers trailed down his broad, dark-thatched chest. "Why don't you come back to the J-Bar-C," she said, her voice gone husky and low. "With me."

Her seeking fingers and suddenly ravenous lips gave him no time to answer.

Which all things considered was fine with him.

Morning dawned gray and cold. Slocum and the drovers, their own joints stiff and creaking with the chill damp, urged the protesting steers to their feet and got them rolling north under a sky that hung down like a low stone ceiling overhead.

Slocum, least experienced of all in dealing with the temperamental beeves, rode lead, out in advance of the huge herd. So he was the first to see it, as he crested a slow rise just beyond the small prosperous town of Mc-Murtyville.

He stopped his paint on the ridge top and simply sat and stared. Then he took the sodden stump of a cigarette from his mouth and threw it into the wet grass. "Shit," he said.

There was no more to say.

Billy Lancer had moved on without making any move against Slocum or the J-Bar-C herd. But then he hadn't had to. Slocum could see the trampled grass and churned mud where the Lazy Lightning herd had rested until early that morning.

And separating him from both deserted campsite and distant Abilene raged the swollen frothing torrent that the day before had been the placid tiny creek called Sawyer's.

8

"Keep those steers movin'!" John Slocum hollered through cupped hands to the far bank of the rain-gorged stream. "Don't let 'em start crowdin' up on the bank!"

A peal of thunder overhead echoed the urgency of his words. The rain came down in gouts, hard and furious now, slowing at times to a light misty drizzle. The bawling of the steers was a constant cacophony. There was no calming them now, no trying to soothe the giant herd. They were scared, scared bad. All the drovers could do was try to channel their panicky flight across the river.

On the far bank—what had been, the day before, a low hummock of ground without a drop of water closer than fifty yards—Cord Blaylock wheeled his white-stockinged stud without acknowledging Slocum's command. Blaylock hadn't wanted to try crossing Sawyer's Creek today. Too damned risky, he'd said. Slocum was in a white hot fever to be on the way. Lancer was out there somewhere in that slate-gray prairie, eating up the miles between his herd and the golden promise of Abilene. Lancer, who had tricked him, trapped him behind a hundred-yard moat of white floodwater and gone laughing on his way. "We're crossing," John Slocum had said, face grim as sudden death. Ellie

Callahan had backed him with a tight-lipped nod.

Blaylock's black gathered itself like a catamount and leapt at a clump of steers staggering up the slippery-wet grass slope. Blaylock waved his hat and hooted. The steers bobbed their great horned heads and scrambled up and over. He hated Slocum, and worse than that, he hated taking John Slocum's orders; but, experienced cowhand that he was, he knew better even than Slocum what would happen if the longhorns started milling on the north bank of the torrent. The steers crossing the stream would be unable to get out of the water and start milling until they were swept away, as a score or more of the beeves already had been. A few bodies could be seen snagged on bushes by the new shoreline downstream, along with a few barrels from the chuck wagon. They were having the Devil's own time getting the animals to enter the roaring flood. If the ones already in the water started backing up and yelling, the part of the herd still on this shore—over half of the more than two thousand steers—would scatter in all directions. As it was, the thousand or so that had crossed were spread out over twenty square miles of prairie, and a good many of them would never be seen again. The cowhands on the north side had their hands full just keeping the herd crossing, and couldn't make more than a token effort to keep it together once it got over. If the beeves got scattered on *both* sides of the creek it would be disaster.

The drive had already come within a few degrees of disaster this morning. Slocum had ordered Cookie to take the chuck wagon across first. The sharp hooves of the steers would cut the riverbottom to bits, even where grass roots held together dirt newly covered by water, churning it into a muddy morass that would suck the wheel of the heavy-laden wagon down like the Devil dragging a damned soul to hell. Blaylock and Bob Ed

Bogen wanted to unload the wagon and take it across light, hoping to rope the barrels of supplies together and float them to the other side, and maybe raft the bagged goods over. Slocum refused. It would take too damned much time, they had no materials to make a raft, and the flooded stream was just too wide to float barrels across with any hope that their contents would stay dry.

Slocum, Carrihew, and the two boys Doug Travis and Charlie McBride had ridden into the river to escort the wagon across. The sturdy, surefooted mules had hauled the wagon slowly but steadily through the racing river, though the water broke against the upstream wall of the wagon like surf on rocks, and the pressure heeled the vehicle dangerously over to the right. But Cookie was as expert a driver as he was a cook, and kept the mules hauling at an even pace, not giving the wagon time to bog or let the force of the running water have its way with the wagon. To Slocum and his companions, and to Ellie on the south bank dividing her time between riding herd on the excited cattle and worriedly watching the procession progress, it seemed that they would make it across without incident.

Until they were perhaps two-thirds of the way across, at a place where Slocum reckoned they had about reached the former north bank of Sawyer's Creek. His attention had begun to drift from the high-walled wagon and splashing mules, and he was thinking about the wetness that soaked him to the waist, and how glad he was he had a box of the newfangled center-fire cartridges his rebored Colts fired in his shirt pocket, where they wouldn't be spoiled, when with an earsplitting squeal the offside lead mule slipped and crashed down flailing in its harness.

The team halted at once, fighting their harnesses and braying. "Shit!" Slocum yelled, and forced the paint to wade faster through water that ran withers-high on the wiry little animal. Cookie was out of the box and into the white foam surging about the wagon with a nimbleness surprising in a man so huge. Daring the force of the torrent and the screaming mule's hooves, he dragged himself along the trace to examine the damage.

Carrihew got to him the same time Slocum did. They dismounted and sent their horses splashing onto the other bank. "Damn," they heard Cookie grunt. "Stone turned underfoot or something. His right foreleg's broke at the pastern."

"Oh Jesus," Doug Travis said. His face was white beneath the sodden sweep of his hatbrim.

As the two youths dismounted to lend what help they could, Cookie battled his way back to the wagon for his immense falling-block Sharps pistol. With a dour glance at Carrihew, Slocum drew his broad-bladed dirk and began sawing at the straps that held the mule to the harness.

He got the kicking creature free. Cookie splashed up, holding the pistol above his head like a torch to keep it out of the water. Fighting the mud bottom that clung to his boots and the current that strove to shove him off his feet, the big man braved the forehooves of the offside wheel-mule and worked his way in to the pole. He knelt, clinging to the wagon tongue with one burly hand, aimed his pistol, and blew the injured mule's brains out with a deafening report and a .54-caliber lead ball.

The rushing current swiftly whirled away the red blood of the dead animal, carrying the smell with it so that the three surviving mules didn't get any more excited than they already were. Grunting, Slocum, Carrihew, and Doug Travis pulled the dead mule clear. The river caught it up and took it away, slowly rotating, as a dripping Cookie resumed his seat and tried to bring the remnants of his team back into a state resembling order.

Their horses now cropping on the north bank, the two older men and Doug Travis trudged along beside the wagon in case something else went wrong, while Charlie McBride sloshed ahead to take the horses in hand and make sure they didn't roll and bust their saddle horns. Something went wrong almost at once. The three straining mules had just got the wagon in motion again when the bottom, which had been the bank the day before, abruptly gave way under the right side of the wagon.

Cookie shouted and snapped the reins. A good hard pull on the right side might have dragged the wagon out of danger before it could overbalance, but that side was weakened by the loss of the lead mule. Slowly, majestically almost, the wagon began to tip to the right.

John Slocum tried to run for the rear of the wagon. He slipped, shouted a curse as his head went under, found purchase for his feet on the slick grass below, and came up sputtering near the rear of the wagon. As he dragged himself over the tailboard of the wagon it gave a heart-stopping lurch and settled a few inches farther to the right. If it went over with Slocum inside, he'd probably be crushed under a ton of barrels of coffee and bacon and gunpowder, and certainly be trapped inside the canvas-covered wreckage and drowned. Without letting himself ponder the possibilities he drew himself up to an uncertain footing, braced his legs wide, and started pitching barrels from the right side of the wagon out of the tailgate.

The wooden casks ranged in weight from fifty pounds to upwards of two hundred. They were slippery, hard to get a grip on. Even in the best of conditions, the largest barrels required two men to manhandle in and out of a wagon, but Slocum picked them up and chucked them out the back as if they were flowered carpetbags. The immediate danger to his life, with the floorboard tilting farther and farther beneath his boot soles with every second, was enough to move any man to prodigious feats of strength. But it wasn't fear for his own life that made Slocum work like a madman, tossing around barrels he wouldn't so much as try to lift on normal days. It was the promise of Abilene, and even more than that the iron-hard determination that Billy Lancer should not get the better of him, that gave him the strength he needed.

He had cleared much of the weight from the right rear of the wagon, though sacks and barrels were beginning to slide over from the other side. He caught up a huge barrel, biceps cracking with the strain—and the wagon lurched. He fell back, the massive weight crushing his chest, driving the air from his lungs with a *whoosh*. Somehow he held on to the tremendous burden, trying to suck in a breath as he felt the wagon begin its dizzying final tip. The image of Lancer's face, laughing, surrounded by a halo of golden hair, appeared before his sweat-filled eyes. With a roar of anger he threw the barrel from him. It struck against the far wall of the wagon, buckling the thick oak. The wagon heeled left at the impact. And then, impossibly, the wagon did not come toppling inexorably back again. Instead it stayed as it was, and began to move forward again, while the water roared and beat its fists against the wagon's hull, in fury at being robbed of its prize. The impact of the barrel had jarred the wagon's right rear wheel from a rut.

Slocum collapsed on a pile of flour sacks, spent and limp as a wet rag doll. He'd ridden the wagon to the north bank, but that was all the rest he'd allowed himself. He'd climbed back aboard the paint as soon as the wagon's wheels touched firm—if not dry—ground, and had been there the last four hours, though his arms felt like strips of rubber and hot pincers gripped his chest muscles with every move he made.

The logjam of horns that had been building on the north bank broke up as Blaylock and his faithful friend Bogen got the steers into motion again. Slocum saw Blaylock call to Bogen, and saw the rat-faced Texan look his way and nod. *Trouble with those two*, he knew. *Soon*.

But there was nothing he could do about it. Keep the cattle moving: that was the whole purpose on this grim, gray day.

The herd was still strung out for a bawling, seething half mile this side of Sawyer's Creek. Far at the rear, Doug and Charlie crisscrossed behind the herd, preventing the beeves from bolting back that way, but not putting pressure on them to move forward. That was done by riders on the flanks. They moved constantly up and down the drove, Ellie and Slocum with White Eyes Merriman, Shag Coltrane, and Lafe Carrihew to the west, Velarde with Andersen, Ray Polder, and Lonesome Dave on the east, escorting the recalcitrant longhorns forward, squiring them across the river and then riding back for more on horses grown treacherously unsure of foot from the fatigue that was grinding down everyone, man and beast alike. Santiago Velarde had run the remount herd across just after Cookie finally got the wagon to shore, losing half a dozen animals to the current. With no one to tend it the remuda wandered all over the north bank. Later they could be gathered up easily enough, but now there wasn't even time for the men to saddle up fresh horses. From the swollen ugly look of the clouds, so near overhead it seemed a man could reach up from the saddle and brush his fingers across them, it was apparently only a matter of time until they burst into a downpour as great as the one of the night before. The J-Bar-C drovers had to get all the steers they intended to move to market across the already swollen stream before that happened.

The day dragged on in a timeless grayness. Once, briefly, after gulping down a tin cup full of hot soup handed to him on the fly by Cookie, Slocum glanced up to see a brief rift torn in the clouds to the west, and was astonished to see the light slanting upward from below, meaning that the sun had dropped near the horizon. Daylight, such as it was, was about to end.

But the J-Bar-C cowhands were a picked crew. Under the careful, skilled guidance of Santiago Velarde and Miss Ellie—with the relatively green cattleman Slocum relegated to taking orders like all the rest—they did their job well. Perhaps two hundred head remained on the south shore by the time Slocum had his furtive glimpse of blue almost-evening sky. Of course, they had lost beeves: over two hundred, near as he could judge, though he had no way to tell how good that judgment was. It was certainly no disaster; a normal loss for a herd this huge crossing a flooded river. A drove on the trail expected to lose a lot of animals, and this one had had incredibly good luck so far. But this was no ordinary herd. With the exaggerated value the Frenchman in Abilene had placed on the beeves, today's losses ran to $20,000—$4,000 out of Slocum's pocket. He felt the loss of every penny keenly. Not for the money's own sake. Four grand was a drop in the bucket compared to what he'd see if they made Abilene with just half the herd that left New Mexico. But Billy Lancer was tarnishing his prize, diminishing his achievement. That cut him to the quick.

It happened very suddenly. Chicken-necked old Ray Polder was in midstream, his lariat coiled in his hand to

wave at faltering steers and to slap his dun mare on the
rump when she showed signs of balking, which was frequently. Like the rest of them he was dead in the saddle,
with the front of his soaked brim fixed to the crown of
his hat with a big brass pin to keep it from hanging in
front of his eyes, and his mare's ears stuck out straight
to the sides like a tired mule's, though she was having to
fight hard to keep her legs under her in the torrent.
Though the rain had stopped here awhile back, not far
to the northwest a solid black curtain lay across the
prairie, and the water had begun to rise, slow but inex-
orable. Slocum had just climbed his bedraggled paint
out of the water on the north side and turned back to see
Polder, his grizzled lean jaws working listlessly on a
plug of tobacco.

Then he was gone.

Horse and man vanished from sight in the blink of an
eye. Slocum just sat there for a moment, not quite able
to comprehend what was happening from the depths of
his fatigue. Then he heard Cord Blaylock shout, "By
God, there he is!" and saw Polder's now hatless head
bob briefly to the surface thirty yards downstream.

An instant later the dun mare surfaced, one leg kicking free of the water in a frantic, doomed struggle to
find some sort of purchase. Later they all figured the
animal had stepped into a hole, where a chunk of sod
had been torn away by the fast-flowing water. Now
every man's eye was riveted on the struggling mare.
Though Polder's head was out of sight his right leg was
clearly visible. He had no *tapaderos* covering his stirrups, and the boot on that side had slipped through. He
was tangled inextricably to the drowning horse like
Ahab to the whale.

With a huge splash Santiago Velarde sent his bay
mare diving from the south bank of the swollen stream.

The bay, with her legs well under her, made strongly and swiftly for the flailing, rolling horse and rider.

Less certain of his paint's ability to keep its legs in the water, Slocum galloped the animal along the north bank. The current was washing Polder and his mount away at a frightening rate of speed. Slocum had a hard time overtaking them. He could see Polder's head and shoulders break water now and again, and one scrawny arm beating feebly. The old guy wasn't giving up without a fight, anyway.

At last Slocum got out in front of the tangled pair and turned his pony into the water. With the current on his side, Velarde had already caught up to Polder and his horse. Slocum saw the dull glint of bare metal in his hand, and then the Mexican dove headfirst into the water.

A moment later he surfaced, with Polder clinging frantically to him. Slocum's paint, drawing energy from some reserve deep inside, breasted the current with strong, sure strides, but Slocum knew already that what would happen would happen before he got there. For a moment the mare's back rose above the churning water. Beyond her shoulder Slocum saw Velarde in his sodden finery and realized the Mexican was trying to cut Polder's leg free of the stirrup.

Slocum heard an encouraging cry from Ellie, what seemed miles away on the south shore. *The mare's gonna make it*, he thought. *She's got her balance back*.

Then the mare stumbled and fell with a shrill scream of terror. She rolled toward Slocum, and he saw Velarde sawing frantically, his knife almost through the stirrup leather.

Then a forehoof caught Velarde alongside the head. He flew backwards into the water, and the mare and Polder were gone from sight in an instant.

With only a fraction of a second to decide, Slocum made up his mind instantly and moved. The water was so deep here that his pony was clearly having trouble keeping its feet under it. Slocum came out of the saddle in an ungainly splashing dive and in a few strokes of his fatigue-weakened arms was at the Mexican's side. Velarde's eyes were shut, with an ugly bruise already purpling the hairline on the left side of his forehead. Slocum hooked an arm around him and, lungs flaming with exertion, hauled him back to his paint. Mounting would have risked unbalancing the cow pony, so Slocum gripped the animal's tail and bawled at him to move. The pony did, instinctively heading for the bank, and in a moment Slocum was lying on the muddy grass in the middle of a concerned crowd.

Someone brought a flask of whiskey. The burning heat revived Slocum and brought a faint stirring of life from Velarde when a few drops were trickled down his throat. Then Ellie was there, kneeling, cradling John Slocum's head in her lap.

"The steers," he gasped, fighting to rise though every fiber of him longed to relax, to slip into oblivion under the cool caresses of the black-haired woman's fingers. *"Keep them damn steers movin'!"*

The men clustered around exchanged looks and moved back to their horses. Slocum shook his head. His wet hair stung his forehead and cheeks like whips. "Don't try to get up," Ellie urged.

"Got to," he muttered. "Hafta—"

"This is it, Slocum!" an angry voice blared. It seemed to come from miles and miles away. "I've took a lot, but no man worth his Tennessee blood will swallow this. *I'm callin' you out!"*

Slocum pulled away from Ellie, lurched to his knees, then to his feet. The world seemed to spin around him.

He struggled to focus his eyes on the tall man striding toward him, with the skinny smaller figure trotting doglike at his heels. "Blaylock," he croaked. "You damn fool, get back to the steers."

Blaylock stopped six feet away. His lean patrician face was a mask of hate. "Ain't enough you lose two hundred head of cattle," he snarled, "you got to go and lose a *man* as well."

"You think I'm happy about that?" Slocum shouted.

"You ain't a fit boss for this cattle drive."

"Yeah," yipped Bogen from behind his friend's elbow. "Anybody'd save a damn stinkin' Meskin instead of a fellow white man ain't worthy to live."

Slocum blinked at him. The fog of exhaustion was beginning to clear from his mind and limbs. He slid his right hand toward the grip of his Colt. "Ray was already gone, you stupid fool. Couldn't do nothin' for him."

Blaylock reddened, and then his face went the white of a steer's skull bleached by the heartless Kansas sun. "You've imposed on decent white men too much, John Slocum," he gritted.

His right hand was already in motion. Slocum was ready for him. He was miles ahead of the lanky Tennessee gun-tough. His lips twisted in a feral grin of rage and triumph as the heavy Colt barrel swung up to bear on Blaylock's midriff, before the other's gun had so much as cleared leather. Slocum pulled the trigger.

And heard a dull *click!* as the hammer dropped on a dud round.

9

He was already in motion when Blaylock's right-hand pistol went off with a boom that drowned the thunder from upstream. He sensed without really hearing the moaning passage of the heavy .44 ball as he left the ground in a desperate dive for the cover of the chuck wagon.

Blaylock's sixgun cracked doom again. The bullet screeched off the iron tire of the offside rear wheel. On his belly in the mud, John Slocum hauled himself on elbows and knees in a desperate slither out of the raging Tennessean's line of fire. Above the ringing in his ears from the two loud reports, and the surf-pounding of his breath, Slocum heard the derisive hooting of Bob Ed Bogen: "Crawl! Crawl on into your hole, you yellow-bellied snake! Won't do you no good with Cord Blaylock on your tail."

Sheltering for a moment behind the left rear wheel, Slocum opened the gate of his Colt with fingers turned to stiff clumsy sausages by cold and fatigue. The wet had soaked the cartridges through, rendering the powder useless. Blaylock hadn't been near the water for hours. He had undoubtedly cleared both his Shawk & McLanahans of the spoiled charges and reloaded them afresh long since.

Another boom and stab of orange flame in the gray dusk. A wrist-thick spoke groaned and cracked six

inches above John Slocum's head. He felt splinters
shower his hair as he ducked lower. "Don't shoot near
the wagon, you damned fool!" he heard Cookie bellow.
"You'll touch off them powder barrels!"

Had he wanted to, Cord Blaylock could have hunkered down and lined up a good shot, and that would
have been the end of Slocum and his drive for Abilene
and riches. But Blaylock was too proud a man for that.
He'd kill his man in a dignified manner, with no
ungraceful hunkering.

Unless by some miracle John Slocum could kill him
first.

The useless cartridges seemed jammed in the cylinder
of the Colt. Slocum fumbled the gun, grabbed it up
again, jacked the ramrod. When the pistol had been a
cap-and-ball affair, the rammer was used to seat the ball
securely on the powder charge. When Slocum had the
piece modified to take illicit center-fire brass cartridges—only Smith & Wesson had the right to manufac-
ture cartridges for breech-loading revolvers, till the
Rollin White patent they held ran out in a year or so,
but that hadn't stopped a horde of wildcat manufac-
turers cropping up to meet the demand for the quick-
feeding shells—he'd left the ramrod in place on the
gunsmith's advice, to make it easier to get spent shells
out of the chamber. Now he frantically levered the rod.
A cartridge slid out with a small rasping noise; grit from
the river had coated it, jamming it and the other cartridges in place.

He heard the soft crunch of Blaylock's boots on the
soggy earth. The lean Tennessean was stalking Slocum
as a panther stalks its prey, taking his time, confident
that his quarry could neither escape nor fight back.
Slocum's lips peeled back from his teeth in a snarl of
rage and fear as he tore open his shirt pocket and

reached for the cardboard box of shells he carried there. *You won't have me easy, Blaylock*, he thought. *Maybe you won't have me at all.*

"Blaylock! Stop that! *Stop it at once!*" Slocum heard Ellie shouting at the gunman, the tone of command in her voice slipping rapidly toward panic as she realized that all her authority would not prevent Cord Blaylock from killing the man he'd marked as his. The other men stood around watching, silent, faces frozen. Whether they held for Slocum or for Blaylock, they were keeping out of this affray. It was between the two combatants, no one else; to interfere would be against the code.

Blaylock's footsteps fell slow and regular as the tolling of a bell. Dull yellow cartridges spilled between Slocum's fingers. He had one chamber clear in the Colt, one chance at life. He jammed a fresh round into the cylinder and slapped shut the gate, then rolled violently to his left as Blaylock fired again. The bullet threw up a gout of red clay from the impression Slocum's body had made in the ground.

Slocum scrambled to his feet, dashing toward the front of the wagon. Blaylock was coming around the tailgate. The surviving mules had been unhitched. Slocum clambered over the wagon pole and pressed his back to the driver's box, rotating the cylinder of his Colt to bring what he hoped was the live cartridge under the hammer. He cocked the pistol.

Ellie had one of her slim navy Colts in both hands, aiming at Cord Blaylock's broad back. "Ellie, no!" Slocum shouted. The navy's hammer fell. Nothing happened. The black-haired woman's caplock weapons were even more vulnerable to the wet than Slocum's modified Colts.

She recocked the pistol and snapped it again. She

might as well have been snapping her fingers. Slocum bent low for a quick glance at Blaylock. He saw his opponent's legs at the far corner of the wagon. Cord Blaylock seemed puzzled by his quarry's behavior.

"Come on out, Slocum!" Blaylock called. "You cain't run far enough to get away, so you might as well die like a man."

"All right, Blaylock," Slocum said. "You called it. I'm coming."

"Cord, watch out!" screamed Bob Ed. Slocum sprang up onto the wagon tongue with tigerish agility, then launched himself forward. Bogen's cry hadn't helped Cord Blaylock at all. It had drawn the Tennessean's attention away from the front of the wagon for the split second in which John Slocum made his dive.

Slocum twisted in midair, landed on his right shoulder, and rolled onto his side, gripping the Colt with both hands. Blaylock fired wildly, and Slocum felt a hammer blow strike his left foot.

"My turn," he said, and pulled the trigger.

Thunder crashed. Blaylock's lean body jerked as though struck by lightning. A fat red stain spread out across the belly of his white linen shirt. His Shawk & McLanahans dropped into the mud as he folded his arms across his gut. His knees gave way and he dropped heavily into a kneeling position. His hazel eyes stared without comprehension at Slocum. He opened his mouth. A bright wash of blood spilled down his chin, and he collapsed to the side.

"My God! Cord! Cord!" Bob Ed Bogen ran stumbling to his friend's side. Blaylock was writhing in the dirt, kicking grooves in the sod with his boot heels. The kicks were gradually getting feebler.

Ellie was at Slocum's side, kneeling down. Her raven hair, heavy with rain, was escaping from the tie at the back of her head and hung down in curtains on either side of her face. "Oh John, are you all right?"

Anger swept through Slocum. He shoved her aside and got up, brushing mud and wet grass from him. "You shouldn't have interfered."

She rocked back on her heels, looking stricken, not understanding.

"That was between us—just Blaylock and me. You should have kept out."

"But I was trying to help you, John." Her tone wavered between pleading and anger.

"Wasn't your place to help." He shook his head. "And you can be thankful your navy misfired. Every man on the drove would have walked on you if you'd shot Blaylock in the back."

Ellie wasn't wavering anymore. Her face was white with fury. She jumped to her feet and faced Slocum with clenched fists on her hips. For a moment she hovered on the verge of screaming at him. Then she turned and ran for her horse.

Dizziness struck Slocum. He let himself slump against the rough swollen wood of the wagon. Something had come between Ellie and him, and he didn't know what.

Or maybe he did, and just didn't want to admit he knew.

They found Ray Polder snagged in the roots of a cottonwood a half mile downstream. The dun mare was never seen again. Ray was buried by the whole crew, in the shade of the cottonwood. He had an old harmonica he used to like to play at night before it was time to turn in. He carried it in his hip pocket, and by some miracle it hadn't been lost. They put it on his chest, with his bloodless, liver-spotted old hands crossed over it, and lowered him into the red Kansas dirt. Ray Polder hadn't been a praying man, so nobody spoke over him. Santiago Velarde murmured something and crossed himself, then grabbed a shovel and started covering Ray up, and the others followed suit.

Bob Ed Bogen buried Cord Blaylock by himself, just about where he fell. No one came to help, or even to stand by as the skinny Texan dug a shallow grave and rolled his friend in.

The herd rolled on into Kansas with the impetus of an avalanche. They crossed several more rivers, lost several score head of cattle, but nothing as bad as Sawyer's Creek. They lost no more men.

For a few days after the killing on Sawyer's Creek Bob Ed Bogen tried to stir the others up against Slocum. They weren't having any of it. Cord Blaylock had been looking for trouble. He'd found it. That settled it. After a while Bob Ed quit trying to talk to the others. At night by the cookfire he'd sit to one side, unspeaking. When he wasn't watching Slocum with his bloodshot little eyes, he was watching Ellie.

If John Slocum had known the thoughts going through the rat-faced Texan's mind when he looked at Ellie Callahan, if he'd had the slightest inkling of what Bob Ed Bogen would do to avenge his friend's death, he would have shot the man as he sat, no matter what the consequences. But Slocum couldn't read minds. Nor could he read the future. And perhaps that was just as well.

Slocum spent a couple of cold nights alone. Then he forgave Ellie—or she forgave him, and neither one got any sleep for a night. When they weren't rutting like minks the two of them discussed what would happen when they had their money and Slocum could come back with Ellie to the J-Bar-C. Though she didn't say so in so many words, it was clear she intended he become a permanent fixture. "Dad's looking for a good man to take over from him when he passes on," she said, looking straight at him in a way that left no doubt that Joe Callahan already had a candidate in mind for a successor. But the *way* she said it . . . There was a bitterness in her voice Slocum couldn't fathom. In a vague way he knew it had to do with what had happened that day at Sawyer's Creek, with the undefined something that lay like a veil between them even when they were locked in a passionate embrace. But John Slocum was not an introspective man. What would happen would happen, and if it happened he wound up as heir apparent to the J-Bar-C, why, that was fine with him.

Wiping red dust from his eyes and forehead with his neckerchief, John Slocum squinted through the brick-colored cloud thrown up by the passage of ten thousand hooves at the figure galloping back along the long line of steers toward him. It was drag for Slocum today, the most miserable post on the whole drive. In most drives, where every man held the same position from start to finish, it was a rite of passage for green hands, kids mostly, to hold down drag. Maybe he was getting old, but John Slocum could not by God see how anybody could stand two or three months of eating dust and wading through cowshit from dawn till dusk.

In a moment he made out the gaudy red shirt and blue neckerchief that Santiago Velarde was wearing today. Like everybody else, the Mexican was restricted to the gear he could carry in his saddlebags and a small satchel and bedroll in the chuck wagon, yet he seemed to have an unendingly variable wardrobe. It mystified hell out of Slocum how he did it, but Lonesome Dave Shapp managed to do the same thing, albeit with quieter taste.

"Señor," Velarde called. He looked out of a swirl of red dust like a ship from a fogbank.

"What's on your mind?" Slocum asked. Since hauling Velarde out of swollen Sawyer's Creek, Slocum had developed a kind of guarded sense of comradeship with the man.

"Have you noticed we are beginning to pass dead steers?"

"Velarde, I haven't noticed anything but dust and two thousand steers' asses since daybreak."

Velarde flashed white teeth in a grin. Then, seriously: "There's something I must show you, señor."

He wheeled his bay mare and loped off at an angle to the drove. Slocum shrugged and followed him. As soon as Slocum emerged from the clouds churned up by the beeves, he saw black cruciform shapes wheeling against the blue-white sky.

Vultures.

A couple of hundred yards away from the attenuated arrowhead of the herd, Slocum saw a clump of what looked like dwarfish priests, standing in solemn convocation over a still shape on the ground. Velarde triggered a blast from one of his huge old Dragoons and the priests spread black wings and soared upward to join their comrades, uttering dry croaks of protest at the interruption of their communion.

"Filthy animals," Velarde said.

Slocum grinned. " 'Thout 'em, we'd all be ass deep in dead critters."

"A necessary evil, señor"—the Mexican holstered his gun—"but still an evil, I think."

Evil or not, the carrion birds had not been long at work on the dead steer. But now that he was free of the smoke screen the drove put up, Slocum could see that the vultures had no need to hurry. Both ahead of the J-Bar-C herd and back along its trail he saw humped forms lying still among clumps of prairie grass green and sweet with late-summer rain. There was plenty of meat available for all the vultures in Kansas.

Inexperienced as he was—though after what he'd gone through on this drive he could no longer be termed "green"—Slocum could see that the steer hadn't been dead long. The hide had begun to dry and shape to the framework of the animal's bones, and was starting to bloat at the belly as the internal organs swelled. "This animal died yesterday," Velarde judged. "Can you guess what it died of?"

"Dunno."

"Disease. Note the hide—looks mangy, *¿qué no?* And the dried slobber on the mouth."

"So somebody's runnin' diseased cattle." Slocum felt anger beginning to boil inside him. It was the sort of thing that brought Texas and New Mexico cattlemen an undeserved bad reputation, so that droves like his sometimes had to fight their way to marketplace.

"No, señor." Velarde swung down from his horse. "*Somebody* is not running diseased cattle."

Slocum's eyes narrowed. He wanted to ask the Mexican what in hell's name he was babbling about, but held back as Velarde walked a few yards and picked up a chunk of driftwood, three feet long and polished silver-gray by sun and water. He came back to the steer and slid it under the bony-ridged back of the carcass, and heaved the animal over with a grunt.

The side exposed showed the raised ridge of a brand on the sunken flank. It was simple: a jagged line that would run parallel to the ground if by some miracle the animal ever got to its feet again.

"I know that brand." At the sound of the new voice Slocum looked around. Ellie had ridden up from her position on the left flank of the drove and was frowning down at the dead beef. "It's from a spread over in the western Panhandle, called the Lazy Lightning."

"Lancer!" Slocum's eyes glittered with an ugly light, like the weird pale light that Plains dwellers know means tornadoes are on the way.

Velarde nodded. "No more than a day ahead of us."

"Why, that means we're catching up to him!" Ellie exclaimed. "We might be able to pass him in another couple of days." Excitement glowed bright pink even through the tan of her cheeks. Her daddy's herd would reach Abilene and the waiting French paymaster first, after all.

"We can pass him if he lets us," Slocum drawled. "Think he'll have a little somethin' to say about it, though."

She frowned. "What could he do?"

"Attack us."

"Remember the stories we heard before we reached McMurtyville, señorita," Velarde reminded gently.

"But he seemed like such a gentleman." She shook her head. "I think you two are worrying too much. And here Abilene's less than a hundred miles away."

Slocum and Velarde exchanged no words. Just a glance. But that glance was sufficient to communicate their understanding that those were liable to be the toughest hundred miles of their lives.

They struck at dusk.

Dusk was a chancy time for drovers. The highly strung longhorns always became apprehensive with the approach of dark. Darkness meant that predators would soon be abroad, stalking beneath a mantle of night, and any unusual sound or smell could panic the jittery steers. Also, as evening began to settle in, the flies came out full force, their biting and buzzing making the steers irritable. The instinctive fear of predators, lone cats or wolves in packs, made the steers want to crowd closer together. That made them more likely to jostle each other, or slap each other with tails swung at pesky flies, which made the animals bellow and leap apart and occasionally try to gore each other. For cowhands who had been in the saddle since before the sun showed above the flat eastern horizon, dusk was a trying time. And potentially a lethal one. Upset steers were prime material for that most dreaded of all cattle drive dangers: stampede.

Afterwards, John Slocum never remembered hearing the first shot. Probably he didn't. The thunder of the longhorns' hooves, the incredible cacophony of their cries and bellows, would have drowned an artillery barrage. And the shot came from far away, on a low hill across the mass of the herd from where Slocum rode.

His first clue that something was wrong was a sound. The bawling of steers took on a higher pitch, and immediately there was a tension in the air, a feeling like lightning about to strike. Standing upright in the tapaderoed stirrups of his high-cantled Mexican saddle, Slocum peered forward through the murk. Far ahead he could make out the high humped outline of the chuck wagon, and in between the figures of Dane Andersen, riding flank a couple of hundred yards ahead of Slocum, and White Eyes Merriman, on swing a few hundred yards ahead of Andersen. A curtain of dust hid Velarde, on right-hand point, from view.

Suddenly a steer broke from the herd, seemingly right in front of Andersen's buckskin. Another followed, and another. Bending low over his horse's neck, Andersen raced after them, to try to guide them back to the mass of their fellows before too many more followed them. Slocum touched his spurs to the piebald flank of his own mount, meaning to go up and give Andersen a hand, and then movement brought his attention around to the left.

A low hummock meandered along parallel to the herd

and perhaps two hundred yards to the west of its course. The sun lay low behind it, painting a blood-red band along the horizon from north to south. Squinting into the eye of the sun, Slocum made out a figure on horseback, galloping along the crest of the rise. It was a big man with meaty shoulders, rifle in hand, wearing a hat that seemed ridiculously small atop his bulk. Slocum plucked the butt end of a cigarette from his lips and threw it away with an exclamation of surprise and anger. There was no mistaking Duke Burnham—one of Billy Lancer's two most favored lieutenants. Slocum reined in his pony so hard it reared, and wheeled it to race around the rear of the herd—and in the process probably saved his own life.

He saw a puff of smoke blossom from the crest of the rise, south of Burnham and about parallel with where Slocum was crossing the herd's trail. Reflexively he glanced along the trudging column of steers to see one of the animals fall kicking onto its side, a red smear across its tawny shoulder.

The other steers screamed at the hot coppery smell of blood and shied away, into their fellows in the center of the column. Slocum saw Ellie racing back along the drove, her hat gone and her black hair billowing behind her, shouting, "Get in among those steers! If they start milling, we've lost them!"

The left-hand riders looked from her to the galloping Burnham in confused consternation. As if at a signal, a line of riders swept over the rise, whooping and firing guns into the air with a crackle like Chinese New Year. In the center of the line, golden curly hair blowing in the breeze, rode Billy Lancer.

Slocum just had time to notice the absence of Lancer's other chief henchman, whip-thin Jamie Sinclair with his brush mustache and gambler's hands, from the half dozen or so charging the J-Bar-C drove.

Slocum recalled that Sinclair had alternated hunting buffalo on contract for the army with dealing monte to earn his eating and drinking money before joining up with Lancer's band. It was doubtless him belly-down behind the ridge, picking off the J-Bar-C beeves with a Sharps bull gun.

Ripping his Henry from its scabbard, Slocum sent his paint lunging forward as fast as its wiry little legs would carry it. He fired from the shoulder, levering in the rim-fire cartridges as fast as he could. He had no hope of hitting anything save by a miracle, but the only hope now lay in heading off Lancer's buckos before they reached the herd. If he threw enough lead their way they might just shear off in time—and while the Henry was neither long-ranged nor particularly hard-hitting, it did hold sixteen rounds if it was carried with one in the spout.

Ellie, either following his lead or struck by the same idea, spurred her big black straight at the strung-out rank of charging men, blazing away with her Win-chester. And from the point position, Lafe Carrihew swerved to the counterattack, his own Henry beginning to speak not much later than Slocum's.

Another dirty-gray balloon of smoke rose against the crimsoned sky. Slocum's gut tensed, awaiting the smashing impact of a rifle ball. Instead another steer gave the puking-coughing grunt of a lung-shot animal and went to its knees with pink blood frothing from nostrils and mouth. The whole point of this bush-whacking was to stampede the J-Bar-C steers, not to kill J-Bar-C drovers, and Sinclair was cool enough to stick to it.

Closer and closer raced the two lines, Slocum's and Lancer's. Slocum's hammer clicked on an empty chamber. Right-handed, he thrust the Henry back in its boot while his left hand drew a Colt and kept on blasting.

Fifty yards, forty, thirty. Still Lancer and his men came on, shooting past the J-Bar-C people to hit the now frantic steers beyond.

Then Billy Lancer dragged back on the reins of his horse, a blood red chestnut with a tail so long it nearly swept the ground. The big animal reared back and lashed the air with powerful hooves. Then it turned as lithely as a yearling colt and rushed back toward the safety of the hummock. With a final spattered volley of shots the other five men turned to follow their leader.

Her face twisted with rage, Ellie charged single-mindedly after them. "Turn back!" Slocum yelled. She ignored him. The paint was blowing hard. It had been far from fresh when it started this charge and was just about out of wind. Slocum dug his rowels in savagely, forcing the small horse to a last heave of effort that brought it straining alongside Ellie's long-legged stallion.

"Go back!" he shouted again.

"Afraid?" she flung at him.

Stung, he leaned from the saddle and grabbed her reins. The horses' shoulders banged together, and both came within inches of tumbling headlong on the sod. Ellie rounded on Slocum, rifle raised high in her gloved right hand as if to strike him. "You damned fool woman, we can't catch 'em now! We gotta try to save the herd." Her eyes blazed into his, uncomprehending. "Your daddy's *steers*, damn it! They'll be all over Kansas if we don't act fast!"

The mention of her father brought her around. The green fire faded from her eyes and she reined in the laboring black. Slocum let go the reins, and she turned to dash back toward the drove.

A few yards beyond, Lafe Carrihew said, "God damn it to hell," and reined in, swinging from the saddle before his horse came to a stop. Dropping the reins and going to one knee, he brought his Henry to his shoulder and drew careful bead on one of the retreating horsemen now nearing the top of the swell of land. He fired. A stocky cowhand with a sunburnt neck threw up his hands and toppled backward out of the saddle. His foot caught in his stirrup, and they heard his screams, high and desperate, as his mount dragged him up over the crest and out of sight.

With a grim smile of satisfaction Carrihew stood and turned to retrieve his horse. Then he froze, staring back toward the long column of cattle spread out before him.

Slocum watched till Billy Lancer was gone from view, then he turned too, wondering what had caught Lafe's attention. And then he saw.

The J-Bar-C steers had become a churning, mindless mass. For a moment they moved in aimless eddies, what the seasoned cowhands called milling. Then like water bursting from a dam they broke out, flooding northeastward away from the sound of gunfire and the smell of blood and gunsmoke.

Slocum saw White Eyes whipping his pinto frantically with his hat, riding before the wave front of horned heads like a sea gull, cutting off to the left toward safety. Dane Andersen wasn't so lucky. He was just chivvying a half-dozen strays back to the main body when the stampede hit him. Slocum saw his mouth open, saw him haul one of his old-model Remingtons out and begin to blast in the hopes of diverting the stampede. It didn't work. In the blink of an eye, horse and man disappeared beneath fear-gripped bodies and razor-sharp hooves. Slocum thought he heard the man scream, but hoped that was just his imagination.

A moment more and the tidal wave swamped the chuck wagon. Slocum thought Cookie Cantwell was doomed, as Andersen had been, but the big-bellied cook was resourceful. He leapt from the driver's box onto the

back of the near wheel mule, slashed it and the others
free with a butcher knife, and went dashing off scant
inches ahead of the horn tips of the first fleeing steers. A
dozen longhorns were crushed by their fellows against
the wagon before the vehicle toppled and broke up like a
ship on a reef. That slowed the onslaught enough for
Cookie, like old White Eyes, to reach safety out of the
path of the stampede.

The strength flowed out of John Slocum like water.
The herd was dispersed; another good man was dead.
Joe Callahan's cattle would never reach Abilene in time
to command the impossibly high prices the French were
offering. Joe Callahan's trust in Slocum had been mis-
placed. Failure weighed on him like anvils.

Billy Lancer had won.

Then Slocum saw a lone figure racing across the
darkening plain, riding hard in pursuit of the fleeing
herd, black hair streaming out like a pennon behind.
John Slocum may have given up, but Elianora Callahan
sure as hell had not.

Slocum was not going to let such a state of affairs
last. Nor was he going to concede a victory to the likes
of Billy Lancer—not until a thousand flashing hooves
ground the life from him the way they had ground the
life from the shapeless rag that once was Dane Andersen.

He looked at Lafe Carrihew, who had mounted and
was patting his horse's neck, trying to soothe its own
jangled nerves.

"Let's go," Slocum said.

10

John Slocum had heard of the sun beating down. He'd known for a long time that that could be more than a figure of speech—tramping the endless roads of mud or dust to Shiloh and to Gettysburg, marching through the rugged mountains or the parched scorpion-ridden deserts of Mexico; even the last weeks herding longhorns across the vast prairies of Kansas. But never, he thought, had he had a more total appreciation for the meaning of the phrase than today, riding with Santiago Velarde toward a shabby little town full of false fronts and raised boardwalks to buy a wagon and fresh supplies.

It wasn't just the afternoon sun that hammered him on its way down and then struck him on the rebound from the cracked hardpan under his horse's hooves. What made the heat most punishing was the utter fatigue weighing down his mind and body. He and the other drovers had been in the saddle two nights and the better part of two days rounding up the scattered J-Bar-C beeves. Ellie, Velarde, and White Eyes Merriman, the most experienced hands in the crew, judged that upwards of six hundred head were irretrievably gone. With the loss of two hundred in the river, and fifty more to general attrition along the route, that meant the twenty-five hundred head that had left New Mexico Territory

121

had been reduced to sixteen hundred fifty, give or take a few. Eighty-five thousand dollars in French gold, gone forever. That weighed on Slocum too, even though Ellie assured him losing that many steers out of a herd this size was nothing out of the ordinary.

But the biggest burden bearing down on John Slocum's broad shoulders had little to do with cattle or weariness.

They'd finally judged that they'd rounded up all the longhorns they could reasonably expect to see again, that morning, and Slocum wanted nothing more than to climb stiffly down off his paint and try to massage enough of the ache out of his thighs to get about a hundred hours of sleep. He'd never been more exhausted in his life.

Then he'd seen Ellie, walking back and forth beside the fire made out of boards taken from the wreckage of the chuck wagon, trying to work the kinks out of her own long legs, her black hair hanging wanton and free down her slim back. Anger had begun to simmer deep inside him. *Maybe I ain't done too good a job safe-guardin' Joe Callahan's cattle,* he told himself, *but I'll by God do right by takin' care of his daughter.*

Face grim, he strode up to her. "You listen to me, Ellie Callahan," he said gruffly, without preamble. "You been takin' too many chances. From now on, when trouble starts, you hightail clear. Understand?"

She met his angry gray eyes with eyes calm and green as shaded pools. "I've been doing my part, John Slocum. And I'll continue to do so, until I've seen my father's cattle safely to market."

"Your father gave me the job of seein' these steers t'market," husked Slocum. "He also set me to look after you."

Slender brows rose. "I'd say I've been taking care of

myself quite well, thank you!''

"In a pig's eye! Chargin' right into those damned bushwhackers—you coulda got a bullet in your pretty little belly, you know that?'' The other men, gathered around the flotsam fire dipping up coffee from a black iron pot salvaged from the wreck, dented like the *Monitor*'s turret after the battle of Hampton Roads, looked up in surprise and then began to look studiously elsewhere, embarrassed at such talk to a lady. Particularly the boss's daughter.

"Damn it, Ellie, it ain't a woman's place to put herself in danger. And from now on you ain't gonna do it. Understand?''

"Is it a woman's place to spend forty hours in the saddle rounding up stampeded cattle?'' she flung at him, hands on hips.

"Well, uh—'' He shook his head as if to clear it. She was taking unfair advantage of his fatigue, trying to befuddle him with feminine wiles. "It just ain't right. Your father set me in charge of this drove. And I say from here on in you keep out of trouble.''

"Damn you, John Slocum, you're talking just like my brother!'' The vehemence of her outburst rocked him back on his heels. He retreated a step, holding hands defensively up between them as tears began to gush from Ellie's eyes.

"Ellie, now wait, I just don't want no harm to come to you—''

"Why shouldn't harm come to me?'' she screamed.

He blinked. This was too much for him. "Your father—''

"Maybe my father would be relieved if I never came back!'' He could only stare at her white, tearstained face as at a stranger. "That surprises you, doesn't it? It shouldn't.

"All these years, since Kevin died, I could feel it every time my father looked at me. The moment the letter came from General Hood, I knew it. My father read the letter and looked at me, and I *knew*. It was as if I could read his mind. He was thinking, I put all my hopes in that boy, all my dreams for the future. *Why did it have to be him to die?*"

Openmouthed, John Slocum stood there shaking his head, trying to deny the black-haired young woman's terrible words. The others weren't even trying to pretend not to listen anymore. They were just looking on with the helpless horror of witnesses to some disaster.

She laughed a strange, dry, bitter laugh. "Shake your head if you will. But I know the truth. If my father could trade my life, here and now, to bring Kevin back, he wouldn't even hesitate." Her lips sketched a savage caricature of a smile. "The best use he can find for me is to try to attract some likely young buck to take over Kevin's place as scion of the House of Callahan. It looks like you're elected. God help you, John Slocum." And she collapsed sobbing to the ground.

He'd known he should have gone to her then. But before God he couldn't. Not after the things she'd said. It was as if she'd stripped him naked by her outburst, herself and him both. He wanted to get to his knees and cower and cover himself. He wanted to run and hide away from the stricken, pitying gazes of the surviving drovers. He wanted to be far away from here, drowning the awful jagged memories of the last few days—the last few minutes—in hard whiskey and soft women. He wanted, at that moment, to be anyone on God's green earth but John Slocum. It was a feeling he'd never known before.

Now, hours later, the words still stung his brain as if

burned in with a white-hot iron. His shock, the sense of unreality he'd felt after Ellie's outburst, had changed with the passage of time. Now his fatigue-poisoned mind had settled into sullen resentment; Ellie had imposed on him. That was it. She had no right to go and say those things to him, in front of everybody. No right at all.

He was glad to be out of her sight for the first time in weeks. He'd meant to catch some shut-eye before making the ten-mile trip in to the town of Leggitt's Junction, which lay to the south and east of their path to Abilene and looked to be the nearest town where new supplies could be laid on. But after Ellie's explosion he'd just saddled his horse back up and ridden on out.

Velarde had come racing after. Slocum hadn't even bothered to snarl at him. If Ellie thought he needed a watchdog, the hell with her, and the hell especially with the damned Mexican hound she set to watch over him.

Another time he might have felt alarm at leaving the herd watched by such a reduced complement of men. But Billy Lancer had won the head start he wanted. He and his drove were long gone toward Abilene by now. And the mood the remaining J-Bar-C drovers were in, any mere jayhawkers who tried to give them trouble would sorely rue the day.

Slocum reined his paint to a halt on the outskirts of the little town. *Danger*, said a voice at the back of his mind. *There's danger here*. Though his horse could barely keep his head up for tiredness, the animal sensed the nearness of cool water in moss-lined troughs, and maybe the bucket of grain waiting for it in some livery stable. It raised its head and nickered its impatience.

Slocum ignored both the horse and the murmur in the back of his skull. He tipped back his hat, scratched the sweaty band it left around his head, and gave Leggitt's

Junction a leisurely looking over. It was unprepossessing. A main street lined with two-story frame buildings —a bank, a town hall, a livery stable, a hotel, a saloon and music hall. A few subsidiary streets wandering from the central avenue in various directions, and all petering out into the bare prairie among clapped-out warehouses and shotgun shacks. It couldn't even be termed a cow town; in those grand bright days of the postwar cattle boom a cow town was a high, wide, and handsome place, full of prosperity and sin—which the residents of a backwater like Leggitt's Junction were more than ready to equate. Not that towns such as this one *lacked* those commodities. But what they had of them was of an inferior grade, like the whitewash that had mostly washed or peeled off the town's structures, and that made them resentful of their fortunate cousins in Abilene, a hundred miles or so to the northeast.

"Expecting trouble, señor?" Velarde asked. Without answering, Slocum clucked to his pony and nudged with his heels. The paint almost tripped himself trying to uproot the clump of buffalo grass he'd been nibbling at. Finally he haggled off a mouthful, favored Slocum with a resentful look, and settled into a slow plow-horse plod, chewing listlessly.

Arrangements for a new wagon were soon made with the owner of the livery stable, who also sold used carriages and wagons he'd gotten from farmers who'd gone bust or immigrants from the East who needed to raise some cash. He was a dour party, medium height, thin and stoop-shouldered, with a curious lumpy nose, like a yam. His prominent pot belly contrasted curiously with his skinny frame, giving him the appearance of having swallowed a cannonball.

"Yeah, I got a wagon might suit you." The stableman propped himself at the elbows on the penknife-

scarred counter of the dim and dingy little office next to
the stable area and began excavation on the hairy cavern
of his left nostril with a little finger. His hands were outsized, the fingers like the legs of an albino tarantula, so
the member was of an appropriate proportion to the
job. "Bought it off a Swede feller, come west with his
family two year ago. Settled down to bein' sodbusters
over by Stone Mountain, needed some seed money."

Slocum, who had not during this or any other sojourn
in Kansas seen anything that could with justice be
described as a mountain, took out his tobacco pouch
and papers and began to roll a smoke. "Studebaker?"

"Nah." Another joint of the finger disappeared up
the man's snout. "Made by some cartwright off to
Illinois somewheres. But it's a good, sound wagon."

The wagon in question was parked in the alley behind
the stable, protected by a tarpaulin. It was peeled off
stiffly, to the accompaniment of great clouds of the
omnipresent red dust. Despite the covering, all the paint
had weathered off, and the wood had dried in heat and
swollen in rain, which meant that many of the joins
were sprung. "It needs some repairs," opined Velarde,
"but I think it will serve us."

"It's a lot lighter-built than the Studebaker we started
with," Slocum observed sourly. "Lighter sprung, too."

Velarde shrugged. "It only has to hold out for a hundred miles, señor. Also. . . ." He let his voice tactfully
trail away. Slocum knew what he was driving at: There
were fewer men to supply than when the drove had left
the J-Bar-C.

They haggled some, with the result that Slocum got
gouged, but less than the kettle-bellied stableman
intended. "I want the damn thing fixed up proper,"
Slocum said, handing over half-payment in advance.
"A wheel comes off in the middle of nowhere, I'll come

back here and nail your ass to that sign of yours out front." So outraged that he withdrew his finger from his nose to jab at Slocum, the owner opened his bear-trap mouth to squawk protest. Slocum cut him off. "I want the work done by first thing in the morning. Or the deal's off."

The stable's proprietor shut his mouth. He wiped his hand on his greasy-looking black trousers. "I'll get right on it," he said in a sullen tone. "I'll prob'ly hafta work all night, not that that makes no never-mind to some kinds of people I could name."

"Damn straight," Slocum said, and left. Velarde grinned, tipped his hat, and followed.

With the usual humility of small-town hostelries, Leggitt's Junction's one and only called itself the Grand Palace Hotel. Like every other building in town it needed a good scrubbing and a new coat of paint, and the porch roof sagged worse than the mattresses in the bedrooms; but it was that, a boardinghouse, or a night under the stars. Slocum had had his fill of the latter, and at a boardinghouse he'd have little chance to slake the hunger for a little hell-raising that had been smoldering inside him since he rode away from the herd that morning.

He clumped through an elaborately carved doorway from which the gilt had mostly been chipped away and let his saddle and bags fall with a thump before the walnut desk. "Need a room."

The brilliantined center-parted hair, gravy-spotted vest, and accountant's sleeve garter behind the desk blinked and shoved a set of wire-rimmed specs up a disdain-wrinkled nose. "Sir, we do not permit non-white parties to take lodging at the Grand Palace."

Slocum looked from the clerk to Velarde. The Mexican let the cigarette stuck in one corner of his mouth droop a fraction of an inch: the equivalent of a shrug.

Because he thought Ellie'd sent the Mexican to keep an eye on him, Slocum had been hating and resenting him all day. That didn't matter just now. He leaned over the desk, grabbed the clerk by his shiny green string tie, and hauled him up until he was standing on tiptoe, his cheeks bulging like a squirrel's as he struggled to breathe. "What this man here is," Slocum said deliberately, "ain't a Mexican. What he is is my saddlemate. And any man who's good enough to ride with me, be he nigger, Dutchman, Chinaman, or Jew, is good enough for you. Ain't that so?"

The clerk's mouth worked like a carp's. No sound came out. Slocum shook him, drawing the knot a bit tighter. The man's face started to go from the color of uncooked dough to that of fresh liver. "Ain't it?"

"Y-yes."

"Good." Slocum let him go. "Now. We want a room."

"Howdy, friend. Buy a girl a drink?"

Even with the better part of a bottle of Old Crow under his belt and the fog of three days without sleep on his brain, John Slocum had to wince at the line. Without looking up from his glass he gestured blearily at the bartender. "Pour a shot of your best cold tea for the little lady."

The bartender, a tombstone of a man whose face was rendered more slablike by its expression of disapproval for Slocum's gibe, came over and poured a glass from a bottle kept under the bar. Slocum swirled a coin around in a pool of spilled whiskey for a moment, then sent it skittering toward the bardog.

"That wasn't a nice thing to say," chided the girl.

That was enough to make Slocum raise his head and stare at her. "You may be a whore," he observed, "but you ain't a common one. Most I've encountered didn't give two pinches of owl shit if a man was nice or not, long as he had money and parted with it nice and easy."

In the yellow glare of kerosene lamps—gasworks were far in the future for the thriving metropolis of Leggitt's Junction—her face was oval, almost pretty. Her corn-silk hair was sorrel at the roots, and there were small pouches of sleeplessness beneath her brown eyes which a heavy layer of paint and powder couldn't entirely hide. Her dress was cheap stained silk, scarlet with crimson flounces, and cut low in front. Slocum liked the amount of white flesh he saw there, and was blearily amused by the apparent genuineness of the outrage in her calf-colored eyes as she leapt to her feet.

"No saddle tramp can talk to me that way!" she yelped. She started to turn away with a swirl of her skirts.

Slocum caught her wrist. "You waited just a half second too long to go into that act, darlin'. Sit down and be civil."

For a token moment she resisted, then allowed him to pull her down onto the barstool beside him. The night-time barroom clamor had subsided at the girl's out-burst, and some of the locals were giving Slocum sullen looks over their lagers. Stomping outsiders into the sawdust was a usual favorite pastime in boonies like this, and an affront to a local damsel was a perfect excuse—even if the honor of the damsel in question had been devalued as often as the greenback. Slocum favored the assembled topers with a gaze made marvelously red-eyed by sleeplessness and dust, with no little help from the booze, at the same time letting his right hand rest on the well-worn grips of his Colt. He was feeling low-down and mean and killing somebody would make him feel a whole lot better, the gesture said. The locals got the message. With a final volley of hostile glances they stuck their snouts back in their mugs and started lapping up the brew.

Slocum turned back to his soiled dove, trying to push from his mind the look Santiago Velarde had given him across the room. "What's your name, darlin'?"

A little vee of a frown persisted a moment between the painted arches of her brows, then smoothed. "Tess," she said. "What's yours?"

"Slocum. John Slocum."

She beamed at him. "That's a nice name. Real manly-like."

He gulped whiskey. He didn't speak. His eyes met hers, and they said plenty.

She blushed and dropped her eyes. "All right," she said in a small voice. "I'm new at this. I'm sorry. I'll go away if you want."

A rat-faced young man with a crimson carbuncle on the end of his nose was committing felonious assault on some popular piece by Offenbach, on a piano that had by the sound last been tuned during the Mexican War. The Grand Palace Hotel had to meet its bills, and since hardly anybody who could help it ever came to Leggitt's Junction (what it was the junction of, Slocum hadn't yet found out), the hotel had installed a barroom and dance hall on the bottom floor to compete with the modestly named Imperial Music Hall down Main Street across from the town hall. Travelers might be few and far between, but there was no lack of sodbusters and Swede farmhands with yellow-white hair, thick tongues, and thicker skulls willing to come in for a little bright lights, watered booze, and negotiable feminine companionship, and to drop a few slugs in friendly games of chance—at least as much friendliness as chance was involved—with what passed for cardsharps hereabouts. The din in the saloon went on pretty much around the clock, which would have drawn some protests from paying guests had any substantial number of the Grand Palace's patrons engaged rooms on anything but an hourly basis. Slocum was tired enough to sleep through a cannonade—he had, in his time—so the noise made him no difference. If it bothered Velarde, the Mexican could go sleep in the stables for all Slocum cared.

But just now he had something else on his mind than sleep. "You got a room here, Tess?"

She bit her lip. Her teeth were white and even, for a wonder. Maybe she wasn't lying about being a newcomer after all. "Yes."

Slocum scattered a handful of silver on the bar and rose. "Then let's go."

She hesitated. He stared at her, more in amazement than anything else. Finally she nodded. "I like you," she said, and stood. Slocum stuck out an elbow. She slipped her pale arm through it and they walked up the stairs as grandly as the Duke and Duchess of Central Kansas. Slocum felt Santiago Velarde's black eyes boring into his back like red-hot drills every step of the way.

Her room was down the hall from the one Slocum shared with the Mexican ranch hand. It was pretty much the same: a sagging featherbed on a tarnished brass stead, a cracked, flyspecked shard of glass for a mirror, a white-painted three-legged stand with an enameled washbasin on it, stained by countless prior occupants who'd sucked up more of the Grand Palace's cheap whiskey than their stomachs would stand for. The wallpaper was decked with floral designs and brown water spots. Here or there somebody, Tess most likely, had cut pictures out of eastern magazines and pasted them up: Adah Menken, a sensation of a few years before who'd died year before last in Paris, bob-haired and dressed in tights, strapped to the back of a horse in the role of Mazeppa that had catapulted her to fame; Lotta Crabtree of San Francisco; and various other glamorous ladies Slocum wasn't familiar with. They lent a wistful air to the room, as if the whore's pretense of innocence but lately fallen wasn't pretense after all.

That suited Slocum fine. Spoiling innocence was just what he felt like right about now.

As Tess walked toward the bed he pounced on her like an animal, strong arms locking around her. She turned her head, panic in her eyes. His hands groped, popped her big breasts right out of the flimsy bodice. He took great handfuls of her breasts, nuzzling her neck. The fear left her eyes and she began to stroke his hair.

Suddenly Slocum pushed her from him. With a small cry she fell forward on her hands and knees on the bed. Without further ado he reached down and flipped her skirt up around her waist. She had nothing on beneath but a garter belt holding up her fishnet stockings. "Now, wait a minute, honey—" Tess began.

Slocum yanked open his belt and unbuttoned his fly. Without taking off his boots he clambered up on the bed and mounted her with the force of a stallion taking a mare. "Ain't you bein' a bit rough?" Tess asked. Then he was thrusting into her, and she gasped.

The round cheeks of her rump were plump, with not exactly the taut firmness of youth. But they were white and round, and they looked mighty inviting to John Slocum. He buried his strong fingers in vulnerable pale flesh.

"Hey, now, take it easy," she protested. In reply Slocum rammed himself into her so hard the brass knobs at the head of the bed banged the wall like drumsticks. He felt the coolness and softness of her ass pressing against his lean hard thighs, groaned, drew back with a jerk, drove home again.

He felt her go moist around him then, and a soft cry escaped her throat. That surprised him too. He took her hard, then, rhythmically, powerfully, as she cried and cooed and writhed around his ramrod hardness. He almost managed to make himself believe that the flabby looseness of her was a welcome change from the oiled-silk tightness and cushioned firmness of Ellie Callahan. With the help of whiskey and exhaustion and nameless anger, he almost did.

At the end she cried out and he collapsed atop her, totally spent. He lay on her, feeling the sweaty warmth of her, as she caressed him and murmured incoherent endearments in his ear. After a while he found the blackness he so badly needed.

He woke in darkness. She was propped on an elbow, naked now, watching him in the shaft of moonlight that spilled in the window. In the stark light of the moon she looked older. The kohl was smeared like bruises around her eyes. Her face was puffy, with the saggy used look he'd seen on the faces of Christ knew how many dozen whores. His stomach turned over slowly inside him as the image of Ellie, naked and writhing beneath that same moon, sprang into his mind. *Maybe I'll have to use that basin.*

"You're awake, darlin'," she said. She ran her pudgy fingers down his chest. "Love me again, will you?"

As she spoke the words years faded from her face, and again she looked like a lost, innocent little girl. Was it all a lie, a whore's fantasy to draw sympathy from the heart of a mark, and money from his purse? John

Slocum never knew. But she begged him then, desperation growing in those bottomless brown eyes.

It would have been better if she'd asked for money. That he could have given her. He had nothing else to give. For all her pleas and fevered caresses, he could not give what she said she wanted. Even when she went to work on him with lips more skilled than those of any white whore he'd known, he could not respond. When he drifted back to sleep she was clinging to his broad chest like a drowning woman to a chunk of driftwood, sobbing.

In the morning he got up, dressed quickly, threw a double eagle on the bed. It was brutal, and even a man so little sensitive as John Slocum knew it. But he could not bear to look at her again.

At the door he heard a quick intake of breath from the bed. A sob? He quickly stepped into the hall and shut the door.

He just didn't want to know.

"I'll meet your two dollars," said the fat man in the checkered vest, "and raise you two." He mopped his expanse of forehead with a mottled rag and took a hearty pull at his beer mug.

Slocum dragged on his cigarette and thought. The fat man with the thin ginger hair brushed from one side of his head to the other to conceal a growing bald spot had a pair of sixes showing, the four of clubs, and the jack of hearts. With one six face-up across the table from Slocum, and two jacks up and one down in Slocum's own hand, the best the big man, who introduced himself as the town's leading and only attorney, could hope for was three of a kind or maybe two pair.

"Meet four, raise two," Slocum said, pushing forward several shiny silver dollars.

The shabby young man on Slocum's left wrinkled his brow and rubbed his forehead with the back of one grimy hand. "This is getting too rich for my blood," he remarked, and turned his cards facedown.

Betting passed to the fourth man sitting around that corner table in the Grand Palace saloon. He blew smoke from his cheroot and pushed forward his own money. "Call."

Slocum turned over his hole card. "Jacks. Three."

The fourth man performed an eloquent shrug. "Beats my measly two pair, don't it?"

The three obviously didn't think Slocum noticed the smirk they passed around as he leaned forward to rake in his winnings. For his part he was having a hell of a time keeping from grinning. He hadn't seen such a painfully obvious gammon since he was twelve, and was mightily entertained.

After leaving Tess's room he'd gone back to the one he shared with Santiago to wash his face and shave. Velarde, who was visibly nursing a potent hangover, had greeted him with a feeble wave of his hand. He said nothing about Slocum's absence, which was wise.

They'd breakfasted on steak and home fries downstairs, then gone over to the stables. The proprietor had clearly taken Slocum's warning to heart. A pimply-faced youth, the owner's son to judge by his long lumpy tuber of a nose, skinny frame, and incipient potbelly, showed them a wagon patched, refitted, and repainted, with clean canvas stretched over shiny brass hoops. Slocum paid over the rest of the money for the wagon and a team of mules, then left Velarde to see to loading the supplies they'd ordered at the general store the night before.

Slocum had drifted back to the Grand Palace to see what was doing. The heavy outer doors of the hotel saloon were fastened open and just the swinging doors in place, in hopes of catching any vagrant breeze that might happen along on this sullen, muggy morning. Slocum pushed through and was hailed by the trio at the table before his eyes had accustomed themselves to the gloom. "Ho there, friend. How about an amiable round at cards?"

He'd gone over and accepted a drink and a chair. "Fine morning," said the man who'd spoken to him. "I'm Milo Cavendish. I'm in investments, hereabouts. The man on your right is our attorney, Clement Stubbs"—nodding to the fat man—"and to your left is Henry Jenks, a man of independent means."

Slocum sipped his neat whiskey. "I'm John Slocum."

He'd sized them up by that time. Stubbs, the attorney, was no doubt what he represented himself to be—attorneys always seemed to manage to stay fat, even in hardscrabble towns like this one—but the other two were preposterous. "Man of means" Henry Jenks was obviously an apprentice town drunk, complete with a frock coat that looked as if it had been used to beat out a fire, a celluloid collar the same hue as his crooked teeth, and a plug hat that had given sustenance to a whole tribe of moths. If that thin deception wasn't a tip-off, Milo Cavendish was. He was no financier. Slocum knew there wasn't anything around here a clan of Piutes would invest in. The man's dress showed clearly what he was—or thought he was. He had on a dove-gray suit, which at least was clean, if thin around the elbows, topped off by a bell-crown beaver that might have been in fashion around the time of the Pierce administration.

It was painfully apparent that Mr. Milo Cavendish considered himself a gambler. And unless John Slocum missed his guess, the other two were playing shill for him. They had him sized up as a stranger with a fair amount of money to throw around, and that made him fair game for the locals.

So they thought.

They'd played a few hands. So far it had been small-time, no raises greater than two dollars. Slocum was sixteen bucks ahead. Which only confirmed his suspicion. He was being set up for the kill.

Now the deal passed to Cavendish. "Five card stud's my game, and I won't pretend otherwise," he said, riffling the deck. "Just to keep things reasonable, I propose we play for pot-limit stakes."

Once more Slocum had to hold back a smile. What Cavendish proposed meant that a player could bet no more than the amount in the pot after someone had opened. In circumstances such as this it was a con at least as old as three-card monte or the badger game. It looked to the sucker as if he couldn't possibly lose much, with a limit and all. But with three confederates jacking up the pot, he could quickly find himself with all his cash and possibles lying there on the table, soon to disappear into somebody else's clutches.

Cavendish dealt each man two cards. Slocum's up-card was the ace of diamonds. He looked at his hole card. A fat black ace of spades. He sipped his drink. Cavendish was showing the ten of hearts. Stubbs had the trey of spades, and the queen of clubs lay in front of Henry Jenks. "You have openers, sir, I believe," Cavendish said to Slocum with a crocodile smile.

"A dollar." Might as well play along with them, see where this led.

Everybody stayed. The sharps were fattening the pot. Slocum's next card was the jack of hearts, and he bet another dollar. Stubbs saw him again. Cavendish was showing the king of spades, and he raised the maximum, six dollars. "I'm out," said Jenks, and turned his up-cards facedown.

Slocum pushed six shiny silver dollars into the pot and called for a new card.

The next card went around. Slocum's was the ace of clubs. Stubbs got another three to go with his spade trey and the seven of hearts he'd got last time. Cavendish got another ten. "Seven dollars," Slocum bet.

He knew what was happening now. Cavendish was using a marked deck, dealing seconds as necessary to make sure he and Slocum got the proper cards, feeding the trash to Jenks and Stubbs and now Stubbs alone. As if to confirm it, Stubbs loudly said, "The heck with this! Let's play a man's game—I raise the limit: twenty-five dollars."

Now Cavendish's smile might have been cut into his thin lips with a razor. "If you gentlemen insist, I'll see your raise and raise *that* the limit. Thirty-two."

His eyes challenged Slocum. These local boys had sized Slocum up as a man who liked to think of himself as one tough hombre who wouldn't back away from a little serious poker playing. For now Slocum was content to play along. He pushed fifty-seven dollars into the pot and said, "Deal."

He raised his glass to his lips as Cavendish dealt him his last card. A hundred and sixty-two dollars in gold and silver glittered in the middle of the table. When the betting was done and the showdown came there'd be a lot more, including every penny Slocum had on him. Slocum would have a minimum of three aces, and suspected Cavendish would do his damnedest to deal him another jack; a full house would make the rube nice and cocky. But Cavendish's next card would be a ten—and so would his hole card.

Of course all that went out the window if John

Slocum got the ace of hearts. Four aces beat anything but a flush royal or straight, and nobody was in contention for one of those. That meant that Cavendish would be controlling that card more closely than any other—

Over the rim of his glass he caught it, a swift back-and-forth motion of the thumb of Cavendish's left hand, the hand that held the deck. He didn't even glance at the fourth card laid face-up before him.

"Normally," he said in a tone of voice that made Cavendish freeze in the act of pushing the deck toward Stubbs, "I insist on getting dealt the card on top, not the next one down. But I'll be reasonable, *cuate*. You show me the card that's really on top, and if it's anything but the ace of hearts you can have the goddamned pot."

Stubb's face turned the color of boiled beets. Cavendish laid the deck down on the table and favored Slocum with a sickly smile. "Now, my good sir," he said, reaching his right hand inside his coat as though for a cigar, "I'm sure you can't mean to impute anything so serious—"

Just exactly too late John Slocum saw what he was doing. Slocum had heard of shoulder rigs before, but never seen one. But that must have been what Cavendish was carrying. Because Slocum had time to no more than lay his hand to the grip of his Colt when he was staring down the yawning bore of a Smith & Wesson Model 1869.

His world exploded in flame and thunder.

11

Milo Cavendish was slammed back in his straight-backed chair as though a sledgehammer had hit him in the chest. A small red hole appeared in his white shirt, just above the vee of his pale gray vest. A pink cloud exploded in back of him, turning into a crimson spatter on the wall behind. He went sailing over backwards, his sawed-off Smith going one way, the deck of cards going most others, the ace of hearts fluttering off the top of the deck.

John Slocum's nostrils were thick with the smell of his own burned hair, and the left side of his head stung as if it were on fire. His first reaction was amazement that he was still alive. His second was that he couldn't hear anything to the left of him at all.

His third was to sweep off his hat, scoop as much money into it in one swipe of his arm as he could, and jump up from the table hauling out his left-hand Colt.

Santiago Velarde stood behind him. Both his immense Dragoons were in his hands, spitting flame and noise as fast as his hard brown thumbs could slip back the hammers. Hip-shooting two guns at once, especially beasts like the Dragoons with mulekicks for recoil, was no way to hit anything. But Velarde wasn't trying to hit anything in particular. His first shot had counted. Now all he had in mind was making the dear departed's friends and neighbors keep their heads down.

He was doing an admirable job. As he spun from the table, Slocum saw townspeople scattering in all directions, diving under tables or out the swinging doors into the street, trying to stay out of the way of the 220-grain balls Velarde was scattering in all directions. Except the bartender. The big blunt man was standing behind his hardwood bar, swinging up a big blunt ten-gauge side-by-side. Slocum slipped two quick shots at him and he went away. Slocum ran out the door.

His paint and Velarde's bay mare were tethered out front, saddled up and ready to go. Velarde busted out through the doors three steps behind him, flinging a last pair of shots into the smoky depths of the bar.

Spilling coins in all directions, Slocum snatched his reins and flung himself onto the back of his little gelding. Velarde jumped into his own ornate saddle. Slocum saw his lips moving. "What?" Slocum said, and turned the right side of his head toward the Mexican.

"I said, we gonna have a hell of a time escaping in that damn wagon."

Slocum was frantically pouring money into one of his saddlebags with one hand, still holding the Colt in his left. Somebody started to push out through the swinging doors. Slocum fired. The bullet knocked a shower of splinters from the doorjamb, and the townie yelped and jumped back.

"Where is the wagon?" Slocum yelled.

"I left it at the store. No point in driving it all the way here and then turning around, ¿qué no?"

"Then go fetch it and take off for camp."

Velarde jerked his head at the hotel door. "But those men—"

Slocum blasted the last two shots in his Colt into the

murk of the saloon. "Leave 'em to me."

Velarde spurred off down the dusty strip of Main Street. Slocum rode the other way, turned at the corner and into the alleyway that ran behind the hotel. An obese black woman with a bandanna tied around her head was emerging from the back door, waddling with the weight of a steaming kettle of water in her hands. Slocum drew his right-hand Colt and shot a hole through a rain barrel at her side. She threw the kettle straight up in the air and took off up the alley like a scalded cat, squalling at the top of her lungs.

Slocum swung off the paint just outside the back door. He stalked inside, gun in hand. As yet, none of the brave defenders of the saloon had thought of ducking out the back. A pot of corn bubbled on a vast stove nearby, and several plucked chickens, goose-pimpled and naked, lay on a counter awaiting dismemberment. There was one open doorway that he judged led into the dining room next to the saloon, and another closed door that probably led to the cellar. Next to that one was a squat coal-oil can. Slocum put a ball through that. Colorless, pungent liquid fountained onto the floor. Slocum scratched a lucifer alive on the stove top, tossed it, and ran. A *whoompf* and a billow of yellow flame followed him into the alley.

He caught up with Velarde a half mile out of town. The Mexican had his mare's reins tied to the tail of the wagon, and he kept glancing apprehensively around the bulging canvas canopy as he rode, checking his backtrail for signs of pursuit. "Are they after us?" he asked as Slocum slowed his horse to a walk alongside the wagon.

Slocum looked back over his shoulder at the pillar of dirty white smoke sprouting from the center of Leggitt's Junction. "I reckon not," he said.

●   ●   ●

Slocum began to suspect something was wrong when the wagon finally creaked to the top of the last low swell of ground and the cattle camp came in view. A cookfire had been made, a stewpot suspended from a tripod over it. Cookie Cantwell stood guard over it—literally, to all appearances. In his burly arms he held cradled a Springfield-Allin rifled musket salvaged from the wreckage of the original chuck wagon. "Now what the hell!" Slocum exclaimed. As an invariable rule, Cookie concentrated solely on his work when he was cooking. "You fellers chase the cows and run off the jayhawkers," he was fond of saying, "and I'll keep the grub hot for you." So far he'd done an admirable job. But Slocum never thought he'd live to see Cookie toting iron while the beans were on.

Velarde, half dozing beside Slocum in the driver's box, tipped the sweeping brim of his sombrero out of his eyes. He sat bolt upright. "¡*A la vé!*" he said. "Look at the steers, señor. They shouldn't be spread out so far. Something's happened."

An ice-cold ball materialized in the pit of Slocum's throat and began trickling down into his belly. He scanned the prairie, mottled gray and yellow by the sun shining down between patches of cloud. He counted four horsemen and Cookie. He'd left nine people at the camp.

And none of the ones in view was Ellie.

"Drive her on in," he brusquely ordered Velarde. He handed over the reins and jumped from the box, dashing around to the rear of the wagon to unhitch his gelding, who was plodding along next to Velarde's mare. Velarde's lean face looked almost pale as Slocum flashed by at a gallop.

The drovers congregated from the quarters of the herd when they saw Slocum racing in. Lonesome Dave reached the cookfire just ahead of Slocum, and with a lurch of sickness Slocum realized that Lonesome Dave hadn't yet changed his shirt. For him to go so long wearing the same soiled linen was as unprecedented as Cookie's carrying a gun while cooking.

Shapp's handsome face was drawn, the wide Indian-looking cheekbones prominent. His eyes, usually half-lidded and deceptively lazy, now sagged with exhaustion. They didn't seem to want to meet Slocum's.

"Ellie's gone," he said.

For a moment John Slocum felt nothing. He simply couldn't assimilate the meaning of the two words: *Ellie's gone.*

Then the realization hit him with the impact of a cannonball. Dimly he was aware of Cookie's gruff voice, almost shrill with outrage and anger, saying, "It was that damned Lancer and his boys. They hit us last night at midnight. Came ridin' through and sent the damn steers flyin' again."

Slocum shut his eyes. "Ellie—?" He couldn't go on. The image of that lithe, lovely body that he had loved so often, so well, trampled, crushed, and cut beneath a thousand merciless hooves, was too much for him. He thought the horror of the hospital at Gettysburg, when the Confederate sentries gave up trying to run off or kill the starving dogs battling for a share of the heaps of human limbs haggled off by surgeons with blunt saws and rusty shears, had annealed his spirit to mutilation and brutal death. Now he knew he was wrong, and the prairie began to dip and swirl giddily around him.

"They took her," Lonesome Dave said in a voice like a winter wind out of the Dakotas.

"That shit-eatin' hound Bogen took her." Cookie spat into the fire. "Soon as they come out of the night he clipped her behind the ear with one of his Colts and tossed her on the back of his horse. Shag Coltrane saw him, tried to stop him." He shook his head. "Sonofa-bitchin' Bogen shot him right in the head."

Slocum's lips peeled away from his teeth. Ellie kidnapped, another good man dead. *Damn you, Bogen! I'll get you for this. I swear God I'll make you suffer! You'll wish the Cherry Cow had caught you, 'fore I'm done!*

"Shag's okay, though." Lonesome Dave gave a rictus smile. "Ball bounced off his thick skull."

"He and Lafe took out after the varmints," Cookie said. "Ain't come back yet, though."

With a crunching of grass and soil under steel-shod wheels, the wagon rolled up. Sweat stood out on Velarde's face. Slocum couldn't make his eyes meet the Mexican's. *Ellie's gone*, he told himself again. *That bastard Lancer has her.*

And what was I doin'? Screwin' some dance-hall whore!

The two kids, Doug and Charlie, had ridden up by now. They were awful solemn-silent. They reminded Slocum of children at the funeral of the first close family member who'd died since they were old enough to understand that death was for real, for keeps.

Gangly, towheaded Doug cast a glance at his stocky pal and piped up, "Can we go after 'em now, Mr. Slocum? We wanted to chase the skunks last night, but Lafe—uh, Mr. Carrihew said we hadta stay and watch over the steers."

"Yeah," Charlie said. "We wanta catch that low-down back-stabber Bogen. And Lancer, too!"

"Can we go now?"

"No," Slocum said. "Lafe did the right thing. We got to keep the herd together. No matter what."

The two boys said nothing, but their eyes called him Judas. "That's the way it is, boys," Lonesome Dave said. "The herd comes first. Always."

John Slocum looked around at the herd, sprawled out over a couple square miles of dusty Kansas real estate. That was the way it was. Joe Callahan had hired him to keep the herd together and ramrod it through to Abilene. No matter what the cost.

He'd never conceived the cost might be so great.

He wished each and every one of those damned ridge-backed long-horned devils would drop dead in its tracks, here and now. Then he could go after Ellie, save her from whatever fate Lancer and company had in store for her—though deep down he knew with awful certainty it was too late. But at least he'd have the satisfaction of seeing Billy Lancer writhe with Slocum's bullet in his guts. And Bob Ed Bogen, too. Lancer's men would shoot him to pieces. But at least he'd never have to face Joe Callahan and tell him what they'd done to his daughter.

And at least he'd never have to face John Slocum in the mirror again.

"Everybody back to your posts," he commanded in a sandpaper rasp. "We'll wait for Lafe and Shag to get back. Maybe they'll know something."

Carrihew and Coltrane got back an hour after sunset. Their horses were lathered and blowing hard, and their faces were masks of red grime where the red dust of Kansas had stuck to the sweat pouring free in the heat and humidity. They dismounted and eagerly accepted mugs filled with hot stew from Cookie's caldron.

Stocky Shag Coltrane, a bloody bandage tied bandanna-fashion around his head, gulped his stew without a word to anybody. Carrihew took a couple of swallows and then paced back and forth, trying to work the soreness out of his thighs. In the dancing flamelight the Silver City gunslinger's face looked even more wolfish than usual.

"Lost 'em clean," he said bitterly. "Goddamn this Kansas hardpan. God*damn* it. Won't hold tracks for shit. They left some prints in the top layer of red dust, but a fucking wind came up after dawn, blew 'em clean to Missouri." He shook his head and tossed some more of the scalding broth down his throat. "Had me exactly one of old Victorio's Mimbreños to track those bastards, we'd a had 'em before lunchtime." He showed his teeth. "Apache'd know what to do with the likes of Bob Ed Bogen, too, I reckon. Cookie, I'd be obliged for some more of your stew."

Cookie spooned him up another mugful. He half drained it at a swallow and fixed Slocum with his pale eyes. "What now?"

Slocum took his time in answering. It was one of those situations where there was no good answer. To press on, and risk abandoning Ellie? Or to abandon the drive, give up all hope of Abilene and Frenchman's gold, and concentrate on somehow tracking down Ellie's abductors and freeing her?

"We press on," he said at last. His voice was scarcely audible over the crackle of the flames, the sighing and swishing and lowing of the sleeping herd.

The others looked at him with faces that gave nothing away in the firelight. The two kids were out tending the beeves, which was good; they'd have raised a ruckus sure. Slocum looked at Velarde, squatting by the fire with a cigarette dangling from his lip, staring moodily into the yellow flames, and by an act of will wrenched his eyes so they met the Mexican's. If there was a man on the drive who could challenge Slocum's decision, it was Velarde. And he loved Elianora Callahan as much as John Slocum did.

Velarde spat his cigarette away. "It's all we can do, señores," he said, and it was as if each syllable were being torn from his guts. "This Billy Lancer won't have stopped his drive for Abilene. I would guess he sent the herd ahead and hung back with some of his men to attack us again when we weren't expecting it. Maybe Señor Bogen even spoke to him, the night of the stampede, made arrangements to betray us."

"Shit," Shag Coltrane said. "Must be just what he done."

"So you figure Lancer's took Miss Ellie north to catch up with his own drove?" Lonesome Dave asked.

"*Sí.*"

"Lancer'd do that," Slocum affirmed.

Cookie slapped his huge hands together. "Well then," he rumbled, "maybe we'll be getting Miss Ellie back right soon."

John Slocum didn't answer. He just turned and walked off into the darkness.

Another day dawned gray and miserable. Even before the first sour-milk clots of light began to spill across the eastern sky, the much reduced crew of drovers had the reluctant steers up and moving. To Abilene.

Their course took them well to the west and north of Leggitt's Junction, roughly in the direction of a town called Hudson twenty miles ahead. By unspoken consent, once the inertia of the drove had been overcome and the steers were rolling, Slocum and Velarde took point, ranging far and wide in advance of the herd, their eyes scanning the gray prairie.

It was Slocum who spotted her. At first he thought it

was his imagination: a small shape lying on a small mound, not two miles from where the drovers had been camped the last few nights.

He reached her first by a few heartbeats. He swung off his horse even as Velarde's mare thundered up behind. He kept his face as immobile as red clay baked by the Kansas sun as he knelt beside the still, naked form.

A pulse was ticking in her wrist, feeble but steady. She was alive, at least. Only when he knew that would Slocum permit himself to look at what they'd done to her.

"*Jesus y María,*" he heard Velarde choke behind him. "*¡Pobrecita!*"

Moving stiffly, as if he'd aged a century or two in the last few minutes, Slocum rose and went to his horse for his poncho. As he knelt down again to wrap it around the unconscious woman he noticed something lying on the ground by her side.

It was a scrap of paper, pinned to the ground by a knife. Slocum reached over, plucked up the knife, and brought the paper to his eyes. Written on it in a flowing cursive hand were the words: "My dear Sergeant Slocum: Your young lady friend proved quite diverting. Now that we've finished with her you may have her back. There may be some use in her yet. Kindest regards, Wm. Lancer."

With an inarticulate scream of rage, John Slocum leapt to his feet and hurled the knife as far as he could into the empty immensity of the clouded sky.

12

"How is she?"

Slocum let himself down to the ground from the wagon's tailgate before he answered Santiago Velarde's worried question. "Ain't come to yet," he said, not adding that he thought that might be a blessing. "She's fevered, too. Must of lay out there half the night."

Velarde looked stricken. Slocum turned away. He had nothing to say to the man's pain. He was too full of his own.

To Slocum had fallen the task of ministering to Elianora Callahan's hurts as best he could. He had cleaned the blood from her thighs with a warm damp cloth, working with a gentleness surprising in such a hard, rough-hewn man. Then he washed her face and carefully scrubbed around her mouth, and the look on his face was anything but gentle.

She'd been manhandled considerably by her captors. Her face was bruised, both eyes blackened, her lips split, but no teeth broken. Her body was welted with angry red weals, especially her rump. Slocum guessed someone had worked on her with the knotted end of a lariat. His teeth ground uncontrollably at the thought of the pain and humiliation she'd undergone, but he had to confess none of the damage from her beatings seemed serious.

He had no way to know how badly she was otherwise. She was still bleeding some, below. Slocum had heard stories from the war, of women who'd bled to death after being raped repeatedly. Hell, he'd *seen* it; no point lying to himself. Though at least he'd never got involved in anything like that. He'd done some ugly things, in the war and since, but he'd never got that low, and he hoped he died before he ever did.

But Lancer . . . Lancer and his animals had *used* her, used Ellie and discarded her on the cold prairie to die. *No, not to die*, he told himself. That cunning bastard Lancer had meant her to be found. He had used her in more ways than one. He was betting that the ravaging of the woman who was at once Slocum's lover and the daughter of the owner of the J-Bar-C herd would force the New Mexico drove to turn back.

As far as John Slocum was concerned he'd won the bet.

Ellie plainly couldn't continue in her present condition. So Slocum's drive had ended in failure here, less than a hundred miles from its goal. He guessed the drove would wait for Ellie to recuperate enough to travel, and then move on to Abilene to sell the beeves at whatever price offered. The Lazy Lightning herd, of course, would have long since been sold to Colonel LeBlanc at his pie-in-the-sky prices.

But Billy Lancer wouldn't be spending any of that good French gold. Because John Slocum intended to ride on alone. A lone man on a good horse could easily catch up to the slow-moving herd long before it reached Abilene. John Slocum would kill Billy Lancer and Bob Ed Bogen. Slowly if he could. But he would kill them.

What happened to John Slocum after that he didn't much care.

●   ●   ●

A nameless stream meandered across the prairie, passing John Slocum on its way from Nebraska to join the Arkansas. Slocum sat on the bank and smoked and watched the sunlight dance on the water and tried not to think.

"Mr. Slocum."

He turned. Doug Travis stood a few feet behind him. The tall, skinny kid showed no fear of the pistol that had appeared in Slocum's hand.

"Cookie sent me to fetch you," the boy said. "Miss Ellie's woke up. She's askin' for you."

He nodded and stood. The afternoon sun had burned off most of the clouds. The brightness of the day didn't penetrate past his skin.

He started off toward the wagon, a quarter mile away. "Mr. Slocum."

Slocum turned back. Doug Travis was looking at him with a strange, feverish light in his young eyes. "It's your fault what happened to Ellie," he said. "When we git to Abilene, I aim to kill you for it." Suddenly bashful, he dropped his eyes. "Just thought I'd let you know."

"Thanks," Slocum said, and walked on.

"John?" He heard her voice as he hoisted himself into the rear of the wagon. The sun made it hot and stuffy beneath the canvas canopy. Cookie had been draping wet towels on Ellie's face to try to keep her cool and ease the fever. "John, is that you?"

He moved forward. She lifted her head, tried to rise. Cookie restrained her with infinite gentleness in his huge paw.

It took Slocum a moment to find his voice. Her eyes were sunken and unnaturally bright, and her cheeks were gray except for purplish bruises and a flush around the bones.

"You just rest," he said. "Don't exercise yourself none."

She reached out and seized his hand. Her grip was surprisingly strong, desperately strong. He settled himself beside her and suddenly she was clinging to him, clutching his shirt in her fists and sobbing against his chest. He could barely bring himself to touch her. He didn't want to hurt her welts, and he felt that somehow he might be defiling her, adding to the deeper damage Lancer had caused her. But she seemed to need his strength, so he put his arms around her, gingerly. Cookie half rose and went out the front of the wagon. Slocum would have sworn the cook's small, bearish eyes were brimming with tears.

Ellie began to cough. Slocum dipped her a drink of stream water from a pan at her side and she drank it gratefully. Then she looked up at him. Her eyes were dry.

"Cookie says you mean to wait here until I heal."

"Yeah."

"*No!*" The violence of the exclamation set her coughing again. She pulled herself up on her elbows, not heeding that the blanket covering her slipped away to reveal one bruised breast. When Slocum tried to push her back down she shoved his hand away.

"This drove isn't stopping, John Slocum. It's going on to Abilene!"

"But Ellie, you—you ain't fit to travel."

She shook her head vehemently. "That doesn't matter. You leave me in Hudson and press on. *Press on.*"

He shook his head. "Can't do it. Sorry. Your father'd never forgive me. I can't say I done too well by him so far, but I won't do this."

"All my father's hopes are tied up in that herd," she said. "It's his whole life. If it doesn't reach Abilene first it'll kill him."

Still Slocum shook his head. Her fingers closed like steel pincers on his wrist. "You listen to me, John Slocum. This herd's going to Abilene. If you won't take it, I will. I'll get up out of this bed and ride till the last animal is weighed and paid for."

"But that'd kill you," Slocum said aghast.

"You have no idea how little that matters to me." Her voice dropped low. "You might be ready to surrender to Billy Lancer, John. *But I'm not!*"

"All right," he said roughly. "We move."

She closed her eyes.

"Horrible," said the man in the black frock coat. "An outrage. It's a shame to our state that these jayhawkers haven't been put down long since."

The old man's snow-white mustache fairly bristled in wrath. "You catch 'em," said the stout blond lady who stood beside him. "Hang 'em all for this goot, *ja*?"

"We'll do our best, Mrs. Hansen," Slocum said.

He stood, hat in hand and ill at ease, in the frilly parlor of Mrs. Hansen's Boarding House in Hudson, Kansas. No less than Mayor Guthridge himself, the old party with the ferocious mustachioes, had overseen the unloading of the delirious Ellie from Cookie's wagon, and seen her bedded in the room next to Mrs. Hansen's own on the bottom floor, under the care of the town doctor.

While the herd forged on a few miles to the east, Slocum had accompanied the cook wagon to Hudson, to see if a place could be found where Ellie could receive proper care. Slocum had made straight for the pitched-roof town hall, whose ornate weather vane of imported French wrought iron was the source of the greatest pride to the town, and gone in to speak to the mayor. Word that Miss Elianora Callahan, daughter of a distinguished New Mexico cattleman and landowner, had been set upon by Red Legs and was in need of proper nursing had galvanized the old gentleman at once. In fact Slocum still halfway expected sparks to fly from the bristling ends of his mustaches.

Informed of Ellie's plight, the stout Mrs. Hansen had trundled out to peer into the wagon for herself. "She beautiful!" the landlady exclaimed, touched to the core of her mid-Victorian soul. "Poor t'ing. She stay my place free till better she gets." And that had settled that.

"Mr. Slocum, I'd like to assure you yet again that the entire resources of this town are at your disposal to aid you in tracking down the perpetrators of this dastardly deed," the mayor said.

Slocum fought a desire to shift his weight from foot to foot, fearful of doing lethal damage to one of the astonishing menagerie of porcelain beasts covering Mrs. Hansen's parlor. He was trying to figure out some way to divert the mayor's helpful vindictiveness. The last thing he needed right now was a posse of armed, excited, and probably well-liquored townsmen riding smack through the middle of his herd. The well-meaning locals would scatter the longhorns better than Lancer had ever done with all the ill will in the world.

"Well, you know, your honor, I'm right grateful to you, but—"

The door to Ellie's bedroom opened and Dr. Isaacs strode out. He was a taut, compact little man with a pointed beard and round glasses perched on a nose of noble dimensions. "I'd appreciate it if you gentlemen would carry on your discussions elsewhere," he said briskly, thrusting his hands into the pockets of his black coat. "The young lady has been most shamefully mistreated, and requires rest."

Slocum winced. "How is she? I mean, how—?"

"I think her fever is a result of exposure, not infection arising from her injuries. If that's the case, her prospects for rapid recovery are fairly good. But it's too soon to tell for sure." Bouncing up and down on the balls of his feet, he whipped off his glasses and began to polish them with an immaculate handkerchief. "I confess I'm more concerned with the scars to her psyche. Medical science is beginning to shed a few glimmerings of light on the ailments of the body. But I'm afraid we are still groping in darkness as far as the mind is concerned."

"Um, thank you, Doctor." The doctor had in fact lost Slocum at the last turn, but in the meantime Slocum had had an inspiration as to how to deal with Mayor Guthridge's zeal.

"You know, your honor, I have to get back to my men. We have to see to our drove before we can go after the jayhawkers. But if your people want to start out, we could catch 'em up later." The doctor was glaring poisonously at Slocum. Slocum ignored him. "We figger they headed, uh, northwest. Matter of fact, some of the boys say there's a considerable reward out for some of them fellers. Say they was Reb guerrillas back during the war."

"What? Border ruffians?" The old man seized Slocum's hand and pumped it enthusiastically. "Thank you, young man. The best of luck to you. Your young lady will receive the best of treatment." And he rushed out of the boardinghouse, his old blue eyes alight with the glory that would be his when his townspeople brought to justice a gang of the hated bandits that had preyed upon Hudson and so many other Kansas towns during the war and the decade before.

"If she is allowed to get enough rest to benefit from her care," Dr. Isaacs added pointedly.

"Thank you, Doctor. Mrs. Hansen." She smiled. She had lovely blue eyes. Slocum fled, just managing to avoid snagging a fat porcelain dog with flowers painted on it off a stand with his hat.

With Ellie safely unloaded, Cookie had driven the wagon around the town square to Markham Brothers Mercantile to check out their stock. Slocum unhitched his paint from the brass post out in front of Mrs. Hansen's and rode around the elm-tree-lined square to join up with the cook.

The covered chuck wagon was parked in front of the store. Parked this side of it was a trim black buckboard with a pair of handsome chestnuts in harness in front and a mighty peculiar apparition on the seat. This was a bird in his twenties or thereabouts, in a shabby black frock coat and a broad-brimmed black hat. He had side-whiskers, a lantern jaw, and a persimmon-eating expression. But what struck Slocum most vividly were his eyes. They were gray, but they burned with an eerie, mad, hating light. Slocum cast an uneasy glance at the long-barreled shotgun resting on the cushioned seat beside the man. He'd seen that look before. He'd seen it one time in Mississippi, on the face of a Georgian from a battery of Armstrong rifled guns, just before the man ran amok with a heavy maul. He'd killed three men and maimed half a dozen others, and took seven heavy minié balls without apparent effect before an officer had drawn careful bead and downed him with two shots in the head from a Leech & Rigdon revolver.

Slocum dismounted and tied his pony to the hitching

rack, uneasily aware of those strange eyes watching him the while. He stepped up onto the raised walkway in front of the store and stopped dead.

A girl had stepped out of the door of Markham Brothers. She was medium height and dressed in white, with a white bonnet tied with a blue ribbon. Golden hair fell in ringlets to either side of the most beautiful face John Slocum had ever seen, an oval face, fair-skinned and pink-cheeked, dominated by two huge eyes the blue of the sky on the loveliest spring morning of a lifetime. Long skirts and crinolines hid her figure from the waist down, but her waist was narrow and her breasts round and high and seemingly ready to burst through the chaste bodice of her dress. In the bright midday sun she seemed to glow, to radiate purity and innocence. Yet as she paused for a minute before the general store her fantastic blue eyes brushed his, and her perfect red lips seemed to part in a smile, showing a hint of flawless white teeth. And though he knew he was imagining things, what he thought he saw far back in those deep blue eyes sent an excruciating twinge through his groin.

Then she swept past. He caught a whiff of the scent of her, pure and fresh as spring water. A clerk in a green eyeshade trotted after her carrying a parcel wrapped in pink paper. He handed her up into the seat of the buckboard next to the madman in the coat, and then strapped the parcel on behind. Without a word or gesture of greeting to the girl, the driver clucked up the horses and sent them on their way. As the light wagon rolled off along the street, the girl looked back once at Slocum, and smiled. He felt his knees turn to water.

"Who in God's name," he asked a loafer sitting by the door with his chair tipped back against the wall, "was that?"

"That li'l gal? Name's Chastity. Chastity Coffin. Daddy's a preacher, up to Calvary." He spat black tobacco juice into the street.

"Calvary? Where's that?"

"Ten, twenty mile along, up the road toward Ab'lene. She come down once, twice a month, pick up things. Ain't no mail stages go by Calvary." He took out a plug of Red Man and scrutinized it with bloodshot eyes. "Mighty strange people in Calvary. Take their religion mighty serious." He haggled off a chunk of tobacco with stained, ragged teeth. "I'm as good a Christian as the next feller, but me, I wonder if they don't go a little far."

Slocum thought of the eerie, pale light in the wagon driver's eyes. "How do you mean, friend?"

The loafer cackled. "Hell, you wouldn't believe me if'n I tol' you. You just gonna have to go to Calvary and see fer you'self." A trickle of juice ran down his grizzled chin. "Which I don't rightly recommend you do. Less'n you wanna run up agin the Rev'rend Hezekiah Coffin."

Slocum looked off along the street. The buckboard was gone, but he remembered those eyes. Had he really seen what he thought he saw? Innocence and lust, purity and passion—a combination like that could drive a man plumb loco.

"I think I might just take my chances."

"Yeah." The oldster spit out the plug of tobacco as if the sting and savor no longer pleased him. "Yeah. Reckon you would." And he got up and hurried off along the street, gimping on a game left leg.

Slocum shook his head. You met some crazy old codgers in these little burgs, that was for sure.

Chastity. He rolled the name around his mind, decided he liked the taste of it. Then he pushed on into the store, to drag Cookie away from the candy before he blew all his pay on horehounds and saltwater taffy.

Billy Lancer was taking no chances. He kept scouts along his backtrail, just in case the J-Bar-C drove hadn't given up. Late in the afternoon of the next day, five Lazy Lightning riders came out of nowhere and swooped down on the herd, guns blazing.

No doubt they counted on easy pickings, with the J-Bar-C crew so badly reduced and with every reason in the world to be demoralized. They were wrong—dead wrong, for some. The treatment of Ellie Callahan had made the New Mexico drovers hornet-mean and just itching for revenge. The raiders ran into a solid wall of fire from the two Henry repeaters, White Eyes' Spencer, and Ellie's 1866 Winchester, wielded with especial vigor by Santiago Velarde, while Cookie boomed away with the Allin and his Sharps pistol and the others emptied their sixguns. In their present mood the J-Bar-C men didn't care if the damned longhorns stampeded again, as long as they drew blood from their enemy.

The longhorns for a wonder didn't stampede. A few head ran off. So did two Lazy Lightning riders, leaving three of their comrades lying in the dust behind.

Two were dead. The third, gray-faced with the pain of a belly wound, proved to be none other than Lancer's trusted lieutenant, Jamie Sinclair. He greeted the J-Bar-C men with a raucous laugh as they rode up to him. "You assholes got the better of it this time." He spat blood into the grass. "Fat lot of good it'll do you. We're miles ahead of you."

Slocum dismounted and walked to his side, keeping a cautious eye on him. Though his holsters were empty and his hands were, too, he was the sort to have a hideout pistol tucked away somewhere. Slocum bent over and looked at him, making sure his body didn't shield Sinclair from the others' line of fire.

"You're in bad shape, Sinclair," he said, straightening. "But I think we could get you back to Hudson in good enough shape for 'em to hang you."

Sinclair blanched. "You're bluffing, Slocum. They'd never hang me."

"You may be right," Slocum said. "They might douse you in coal oil and set you afire. They do that to rapists sometimes, I hear."

Sinclair turned green. Then he laughed. "I'm a dead man anyway. You'd never get me back to town."

"Don't it bother you that your friends ran off and left you, Sinclair?" Lonesome Dave asked. He'd climbed off his horse and was laboriously reloading his Colts.

"Naw." Sinclair shook his head, then winced. Motion obviously caused him pain. "Billy Lancer's a child of destiny, just like he always says. He's not going to turn aside for the likes of me. But shit, I had some high old times with him. Had to end sometimes. It's enough for me to know he's going to win, to rub your stinking noses in the dirt."

He looked around at his captors with a ragged leer. "Hey, we had us a high old time with that little black-haired lady of yours. She could sure roll it when you plugged into her, 'specially when old Duke touched her up with a rope end. And that Bogen friend of yours—didn't he know how to give her what for! Said she tried to shoot his friend Blaylock in the back, so he'd give it to her, right up the back. She squalled like a catamount then, let me tell—"

Santiago Velarde stepped forward. Steel glinted in his right hand. He grabbed Jamie Sinclair by the hair in mid-sentence, hauled his head back, and slit his throat with a single neat motion. Blood gushed in a long arc. Sinclair thrashed for a moment, then fell limp. The front of his shirt was soaked in blood.

Velarde stepped back, looking down at the dead man, his dripping dagger in hand. "I'm sorry, señores. I could not permit him to speak so of Señorita Elianora. It was a *pundonor*—a point of honor."

Slocum stepped up to him, looked into his eyes for a moment, then gripped the Mexican's shoulder.

"Glad we didn't have to waste another ball on the sonofabitch," said Lonesome Dave.

Thunder split the sky across. The rain-wracked prairie glowed briefly blue-white. The figures of nearly two thousand steers stood out for an instant in stark contrast, churning, struggling, heads lifted and eyes rolling in terror, like some ancient woodcut of the damned in hell. Then all was darkness.

And it was indeed like one of the torments of Dante's damned, trying somehow to keep the herd together, to keep it moving, to keep the steers from beginning to mill, when the driving rain drew a thick black curtain over everything, ripped sporadically by blades of lightning. Soaked to the skin, hammered by rain so furious that it stung the exposed skin of hands and face, John Slocum fought desperately to keep the mighty herd intact. Sometimes he found himself surrounded by the longhorns, their bawling just audible above the pounding of the rain and the lightning's cannonade. Other times the fleeting bursts of illumination caught him alone, with the tide of frightened cattle eddying away from him. He caught glimpses of the others now and then, Doug Travis, his young face set and grim, determined not to show the fear Slocum knew he must feel; Lonesome Dave, eyes half-lidded and lazy, as if in ruining his garments by rain and mud the storm had worked all the harm to him it could, and nothing more it might do to him would trouble him in the least; Cookie in the box of the wagon, which was lurching over the prairie like the Flying Dutchman, heeling this way and that to the wind and the rise and fall of the land like a ship on a stormy sea.

In the intervals of blackness he saw the face of Chastity Coffin.

For two nights now she'd haunted his sleep. Not even in daylight—or the roaring blackness that had swallowed today's sun—could he entirely keep her from his mind's eye.

He had tried to tell himself that it was disloyal to Ellie to think of the preacher's daughter with the hair like spun gold, that he was compounding his crime in whoring while Ellie was whisked away to humiliation, degradation, and pain. But somehow the wickedness of it made the thought of her, that ripe and taut young body, as innocent and inviting as ripe fruit in that pure white garment, more beguiling and demanding still.

He was near her now. He could practically feel her burning like a beacon in Calvary, somewhere ahead in the storm, two miles or three. And now, as his pony reared and sidestepped and slipped in mud to avoid a blind swipe of five-foot horns he was detached, allowing the paint to find his own footing and forge on again. He was trying to summon up Ellie's face, to lay the image of the demon in white and blue.

But he couldn't. It was as if Ellie were a million years in the past. Someone he'd read about in a book, heard of in a story.

Chastity. He had to see her again. Perhaps that night, if the storm abated enough for him to leave the herd. Perhaps they had come farther than they thought. They might be on the very outskirts of Calvary. He could be in her presence in hours, maybe even minutes.

What makes you think she'd have anything to do with the likes of you? asked the skeptic in him. *A half-drowned muskrat of a saddle tramp got no call expecting the favor of a high and fancy lady.*

But he knew better. He'd seen it in those eyes. He knew he had.

Though he wouldn't have recognized the reference, Chastity Coffin had become his Grail—just as Abilene was. She had not supplanted that other goal. But he was just as driven to win through to her, to confirm the promise of her eyes and ripe young body, as he was to beat Billy Lancer to Abilene and reap its golden reward.

Through the snare-drum rattle of rain on his hat he became aware that someone was calling his name. Wolf-lean Lafe Carrihew had somehow found him in the tempest and was shouting and waving his arm. Slocum shouted back, turned his paint away from the torrent of living flesh that was the herd.

All he could hear of Carrihew's voice was an occasional syllable, meaningless above the unbelievable din. But then a lightning bolt arched overhead, and Slocum had no need to hear the gunman. He saw for himself what had excited Carrihew.

Dead steers. Not a few lying by the wayside, as they had seen that day Lancer's men stampeded the drove, but hundreds—thousands maybe, a sea of corpses extending in all directions as far as the curtains of rain would permit vision to range.

His pony's scream rang shrill in his ears, and the animal reared, hooves lashing at the air. Almost at its feet he saw the sprawled carcass of a steer, tongue bulging from lifeless lips, eyes rolled up as if to stare at the gaping cleft in its skull. He saw the Lazy Lightning brand on its flank, and then the light was gone again.

Carrihew's horse crab-stepped up next to Slocum's. "They're all over the place." His voice sounded small and distant, though he was yelling at the top of his lungs, practically in Slocum's ear. "They all been butchered somehow. Shot, poleaxed, throat slit—ever' one of 'em."

Tipping his head forward so that water would run freely off the brim, Slocum peered at the hellish scene in the intermittent glare of the lightning. *Good thing it's rainin'*, he thought. *Otherwise the smell of blood'd drive our steers plumb crazy.*

White Eyes hove up through the rain. His face was pale and peaked beneath his hat brim. "What the hell happened here?" he shouted, leaning far out of his saddle to make himself heard.

Slocum could only shake his head.

He started riding toward the front of the herd. It was treacherous going, with the ground slick and dead steers everywhere. Once a panicked steer ran right across his path and narrowly missed goring the paint with its wideswept horns. Somehow in the tumult Slocum found Velarde, who had been riding point. The formalities of position had long since become hopelessly confused in the cloudburst, but Velarde was still more or less at the front of the drove.

He confirmed what Slocum had feared. "We have to either find a clear path through all these carcasses or go around, señor. Half of our steers will break their legs stumbling over bodies. And sooner or later they'll start smelling death, and we'll never control them after that."

Slocum turned back, blundered into White Eyes, and told him to pass the word to try to get the herd stopped. Then Slocum caught up with Velarde again and together they rode out in advance of the herd, seeking some avenue through the field of carcasses.

The land sloped gently to a wide, mound-shaped hill in front of them—that much they could make out through the shifting veils of rain. They made for the hilltop. It would offer the best vantage point to survey the scene, and also Slocum glimpsed what looked, unaccountably enough, like a small stand of trees at the very crown. *Damn*, he told himself. *I'd sell my soul to get out of this rain. Even a little bit, even for a minute.*

The rain came down heavier than before, so that Slocum could scarcely see ten feet ahead. With the mud turned the consistency of crude oil underfoot, and the grass beaten flat by the rain and defying purchase, even the slow slope was an obstacle to the horses. They seemed to lose five feet for every ten they climbed. Slocum found it took all his attention to keep his plucky but exhausted little paint progressing at all.

When he reckoned they were almost to the top of the hill, he heard Velarde say, "I don't think those are trees, señor."

"What the hell else would they be?"

Lightning flamed, searing the prairie nearby. "*¡Madre de Dios!*" Velarde whispered, and somehow Slocum heard him clearly.

They were not trees. Not natural ones, at least. Three tall crosses stood at the crown of the moundlike hill. From each was suspended the naked body of a man.

Crucified.

13

"Lancer!"

The exclamation tore itself from Slocum's lips and was whipped away by the wind. He knew the men who hung frozen in the attitudes of slow and excruciating death, their skin blue-white, their bodies twisted, sinew and corded muscles standing out in bold relief as if still tensed in the desperate losing battle with gravity, tongues extended, purple and swollen from slow suffocation.

The crosses were made from railroad ties, crossbeam laid across upright to form a rude T. On the left, nailed through wrists and feet, was Bob Ed Bogen, his face scarcely recognizable, set as it was in a shriek of terminal agony. On the right hung the barrel-chested Englishman, John Burnham, known as the Duke. His massive strength had evidently enabled him to hold out longer than his executioners found convenient; his shinbones had been smashed, by sledge or crowbar, and shards of bright bone stuck out of the mangled meat of his legs. The wounds, like those of the railroad spikes driven through his extremities, were strangely bloodless. The rain had washed the blood away.

Centerpiece of the grotesque tableau was Billy Lancer. His golden curly hair now hung in lank strands around a marble-white face. His hazel eyes bulged from their sockets, and his tongue jutted from his mouth like the tongues of the steers he had been guiding to market in Abilene, and which now lay slaughtered all around. The flesh of his arms was shredded around the thick spikes driven between the bones of his forearms. He had fought to the very last to free himself. It had done no good.

Behind himself, John Slocum heard the sound of retching. The terrible scene was too much for Santiago Velarde.

As for himself . . . John Slocum had sworn to exact a horrible vengeance on Billy Lancer and Bob Ed Bogen. Here it had been done for him, and all he had to complain about was that he had been robbed of the pleasure of seeing them die. John Burnham he had little enough against, save that he had been Lancer's lieutenant, which meant that he too probably richly deserved the fate that had overtaken him. All things considered, Slocum should have been elated to see his most hated enemies brought to this.

All the same, he wasn't looking forward to the next time he closed his eyes to sleep. Nor the next. Nor the next after that.

The fury of the storm could not endure. Some time after Slocum and Velarde had ridden off the hilltop to rejoin the drove the rain stopped with the abruptness of a curtain lifting. The cover of thick leaden clouds above immediately began to dissipate, and the J-Bar-C drovers were astounded to see the light of mid-afternoon, dazzling to eyes accustomed to the pitlike blackness of the storm, shining through the rifts from above.

The herd had been brought to a stop in a great hollow beneath the hill. The storm had exhausted the steers.

They stood—miserable, shivering, and dripping, their horned heads low, their tails between their legs. An unknown number had disappeared during the cloudburst. Slocum was immune to their loss. He still lusted after the Frenchman's gold, but this drive had become a personal quest for him, a struggle against fate, and if he stumbled into Abilene with one spavined steer able to stagger to the loading gate he would count himself the victor.

A brief debate broke out as to what to do about the ghastly relics on the hill. "We cain't just leave 'em out here fer the crows to peck their eyes and the coyotes to chew on 'em," White Eyes Merriman maintained staunchly. " 'Tain't Christian."

"Ain't got time, old man," Slocum said.

Merriman was adamant. "It's the least we can do. I ain't sayin' they didn't deserve it. But, damnation, Johnny, we cain't just leave 'em!"

Slocum walked over to the chuck wagon, rooted around under the sodden canopy, and returned. "Here," he said, offering something to the old ex-scout. "You'll need this."

"What I want with a crowbar, John?"

"To pry them stiffs down off the crosses with."

White Eyes went gray and turned away, making choking noises.

"Anybody else volunteer for burial detail?" Slocum asked. "Thought not. Come on, boys, let's get them steers movin' while we still got light." He went and tossed the crowbar back in among the barrels and sacks. When he turned he saw Doug Travis riding hell-for-leather down the flank of a rise neighboring the hill of the crosses.

He arrived out of breath, as if he'd run the whole

way. "Mr. Slocum," he panted. "That town, a mile or so ahead—" He paused and sucked in great swallows of air.

"What about it?" Lonesome Dave demanded. He'd gotten a fresh shirt out of his saddlebags, which he'd providentially tossed in the wagon when the clouds broke open, and was buttoning it up.

"There—there's a mess of people marchin' out of it. Some ahorse, most of 'em on foot." He glanced back to the summit he'd just left, where his pal Charlie lay belly-down watching the approaching mob. "Looked like they was armed."

Slocum felt tired. He'd hoped the religious folk of Calvary would be too caught up with spiritual matters to care about the cattle drive coming through their vicinity. Chastity sprang to mind—the way those round breasts pushed out the front of her dress. He forced the thought away. "Mount up, boys."

"What do we do, John?" White Eyes asked.

"Start the herd rollin'."

"And if them sodbusters make trouble?"

Shag Coltrane answered for Slocum. "We finish it for 'em."

The steers were reluctant to get going again. Once under way, they proved surprisingly tractable. They were just too worn out to raise their usual hell.

As the others rode back and forth shouting at the steers and waving their hats to make them go, Slocum rode up the hill to where Charlie still lay in the mud, spying on the people coming out of Calvary. "What do you see?"

Charlie pointed. The land flattened on the other side of the rise. About a mile away across the plain stood a town that seemed to glow with its own white light in the afternoon sun. Even at this distance Slocum had the impression of neatness, precision, utter order and cleanliness in its streets and pitched-roof buildings.

Midway between the last low hills and the town stood a crowd of men. They looked to be over a hundred strong. Several were mounted, and most of them carried what looked from here like farm implements of various types: hoes, shovels, pitchforks, axes. Slocum thought he saw some long arms, rifles or shotguns, but could not be sure.

"They just marched out of there and stopped dead, Mr. Slocum," Charlie McBride said. "What are we gonna do?" There was no apprehension in his voice. He was merely asking for information. It was apparent to Slocum that after what the boy had been through the last few weeks he didn't find the ragged collection of townspeople standing in their way very ominous.

"We ride."

They rode. They ran the herd to the west of the lower hill, well away from the hill with the three crosses. At Slocum's orders the herd swung wide, so as to make clear that it was to pass no nearer than necessary to the town. A roaring, whitecapped river, which they had crossed earlier that day as a stream, ran here close to the town, an impassable barrier to the west. Likewise another stream swollen beyond hope of passage lay two miles east. So the drove could not entirely avoid the town. Still, Slocum meant to do all he could to reassure the inhabitants that his animals posed no threat to the settlement or its surrounding fields.

"Don't like it." Lafe Carrihew pulled his strapping bay alongside Slocum's smaller paint. His long-boned face showed concern. It wasn't something Slocum expected from the hard-bitten gunman. "They just stand there. Not even sayin' nothin'—the wind's behind 'em, we'd hear 'em if they so much as spoke." He shook his head. "There's gonna be trouble."

"We're ready," Slocum said.

Lafe raised his head and looked at the townsmen standing in silent ranks ahead. "Yeah."

Two hundred yards separated the silent crowd from the first animals of the J-Bar-C. There was a stir, and the ranks of the townsmen parted. A man on a pale horse passed through and rode toward Slocum at a deliberate walk. Slocum clucked up his paint to a faster walk. He wanted to be in front of the herd when he met the other. But neither would he be seen to hurry.

The other man stopped his horse ten yards shy of Slocum. Slocum halted at the same time. "Turn back," the man said in a voice that boomed like thunder.

He was a tall man, taller perhaps than John Slocum. His frame was gaunt, encased in a long black frock coat, black vest and trousers, black shoes, and he had a wide black hat on his head. His head was long and narrow, with striking bones, all jutting ridges and deep shadowed hollows. And the eyes. They were black, but they burned like fire. They were eyes that knew no softness, no mercy. Slocum was reminded of the pale-eyed man he'd seen in the box of the buckboard in Hudson. They were as inoffensive as a lamb's compared to the eyes of this stark man.

"My name's John Slocum. I'm takin' this herd to railhead in Abilene. We don't mean no harm. All we want is to pass by your town and be on our way."

"It matters not what you name yourself. You shall not pass."

Slocum let his eyes slide past the man. His followers stood, still, unspeaking, leaning on their implements. Watching.

"We got to. You see the way the rivers are." He

nodded his head from side to side. The torrents could be seen shining like silver bands in the waning sun. "We have to pass near your town. But you got nothin' to fear from us."

The other looked at Slocum as if from a vast height. Slocum wondered how old he was. The hair that hung long from beneath his hat was dark, shot well through with gray, yet an energy as of a young man radiated from this strange figure. "It matters not," the tall man said. "You may halt where you are and await the receding of the waters. But we will not permit you to bring your pollution to Calvary."

Slocum was beginning to be nettled. "Look, mister—you're Reverend Coffin, ain't you?"

A solemn nod. "I am he."

"Well, look, Reverend, we don't aim to do nothin' to you or your precious town. But we cain't wait for the water to go down. We got to be in Abilene soon's we can."

A rail-thin arm shot out, pointing past Slocum's right shoulder. "You saw how those others who tried to defile Calvary with their diseased herd were punished. Do you not fear God's wrath, John Slocum?"

"I don't know nothin' about God's wrath, Reverend. But them steers of ours are clean."

"They are an abomination! As you, your ways are an abomination. You shall not be suffered to pass."

"Mister, I ain't no preacher. Don't know nothin' about heaven, or the wrath of God you seem so hipped on. But I know me and my men have gone through six hundred miles of hell to bring this drove this far. We ain't turnin' back, and we ain't stoppin'."

"Blasphemer!" howled the preacher. "Turn back at once! Turn back or my people shall smite you as the children of Israel smote the Canaanites and the

Amorites, hip and thigh! We shall hamstring your horses and burn your chariot with fire!''

"If that's the way you want it, Reverend." John Slocum turned his horse around and rode back toward the drove.

As he approached the leading steers he gave a piercing whistle. It was the signal even the most peacably inclined of the J-Bar-C men were hoping to hear. It seemed that they had been chivvied from pillar to post since the battle with the jayhawkers; struck, but seldom getting to strike back. If these Bible-beating yahoos thought they could impose on them, nothing would please the drovers more than teaching them otherwise.

All the cowhands rode forward, leaving the steers and the remuda herd to fend for themselves. The animals were still staggering from the storm. They probably would not get out of hand before the wranglers could settle these sodbusters' hash and get back to them. The seven riders formed up on either side of John Slocum, three on his left and four on his right. Cookie Cantwell swung out of the box of his wagon to trudge alongside, his Springfield in hand, his wrist-busting Sharps pistol stuck through his belt alongside his butcher knife. All weapons had been cleaned and reloaded since the rain had stopped. Those men who carried long arms held them ready in their hands.

Slocum turned back to face the citizens of Calvary. He thought he saw an uneasy shifting in their ranks. For untrained foot soldiers to stand the charge of cavalry, no matter how few and draggle-tailed, was a difficult thing. "At the walk, men," he said. "Don't fire before I do."

He was proud of them then, before God he was: Lafe Carrihew on his left, leaning forward eagerly in his saddle, his Henry held high like a cavalry saber; wise old White Eyes, humming to himself, Spencer across his saddlebow; Shag Coltrane bareheaded but for his filthy bandage on the flank. At the right end of the line rode Lonesome Dave Shapp, mustache freshly waxed, fresh linen gleaming like the houses of Calvary, whistling as he rode; Doug Travis, bowstring taut, and Charlie McBride beside him as solid and self-assured as a veteran. On Slocum's right rode Santiago Velarde, his silver crucifix hanging prominently outside his shirt. He tipped the barrel of Ellie's Winchester to the brim of his sombrero and grinned at Slocum. Slocum threw him a grin and a salute. "Santiago," he said, "there's no man I'd be prouder to have ride beside me."

"Gracias, señor. The same for me, as well."

When they were a hundred fifty yards from the unspeaking mob, Slocum said, "Trot." The drovers obeyed at once, and the line only wavered momentarily before straightening out as true as Jeb Stuart's finest.

As the distance between the two groups of men diminished, Slocum felt a brief twinge. The sodbusters were uncommon steady, he had to give them that. But they'd break and run when the J-Bar-C boys charged through.

"Tell your boys to stand aside, Reverend," he called. "Or I won't answer for what comes next."

"On your own head be it, O son of Sodom," came the ringing reply.

Slocum raised his Henry high overhead. The day seemed to pause and hold its breath. Then: *"Charge!"*

The Henry swung down. The line of riders broke into a gallop, bearing swiftly down upon the unmoving men of Calvary. Slocum thought, *My God, their eyes! They all have the same damn crazy eyes!*

The Reverend Hezekiah Coffin raised scarecrow arms above his head. "Forward! *For the Lord thy God is the Lord of Hosts!*"

The mouths of the waiting men, which had stayed so resolutely shut, opened as one to a single resounding roar of hatred and fury. Like an avalanche they began moving forward, slowly at first, then gathering speed to a headlong charge into the very faces of the enemy horsemen, holding their tools like pikes to smite the foe.

A pistol shot cracked from the midst of the howling mob. Far behind the line of riders Cookie Cantwell pressed the trigger of his rifled musket. The balding head of a massive man in the front rank, whose belly far overhung the rope that held up his black britches, snapped back. Blood and brains sprayed over those behind. From the midst of his wild wiry beard he gasped "Jesus!" and fell. The others came on, trampling his body into the mud.

Slocum raised the Henry and fired. A young man went to his knees, a shotgun with a wire-wrapped old barrel slipping from his hands. He shook his fist at Slocum, coughed blood, and died as the fire of the other J-Bar-C riders winnowed the Calvary ranks like a scythe.

The Calvary men were singing now, shots popping sporadically from their ranks, none coming near Slocum. As his heart and his pony's hooves drummed ever faster, Slocum realized what it was that Lonesome Dave Shapp was whistling: *Garryowen. Never thought I'd see the day I'd ride to battle to a damned Yankee song*, he thought.

The lines met. Slocum caught a glimpse of a haggard, bearded face, screaming as its owner went down beneath his horse's hooves. He was firing the Henry frantically; the men of Calvary were falling on every side. Yet they came on.

From the corner of his eye he saw a flash of movement. He ducked. A shovel struck him glancingly on the temple, bounced off his left shoulder. His left arm went numb. He flipped the Henry to that side, fired into the shouting face of the shovel wielder as the man raised his weapon to strike again. The muzzle flash blackened the face and set the man's beard ablaze. He fell.

Someone else struck at Slocum with a hoe. He fended the blow with the Henry, then weaved desperately to the side to avoid a brick hurled at his head. He fired again but didn't know if he hit anyone.

Off to his right he saw Lonesome Dave. Like Slocum the dandy was surrounded by a sea of angry, singing men. He held an army Colt in either hand, firing coolly left and right.

Slocum saw a brawny arm cock back and shouted a warning. Shapp glanced his way, an easy smile on his lips. The arm snapped forward and a flung pitchfork struck Lonesome Dave right below the breastbone.

Lonesome Dave looked down at his own bright scarlet blood irrevocably spoiling his fresh white shirt. With a look of annoyance on his handsome face he raised one of his pistols and shot down the man who'd thrown the implement. Then he toppled from his saddle and was lost to view.

Strong hands clutched at Slocum. He hacked with his Henry as if it were a sword, felt bone crunch. Blood spattered his right side. A ragged man leapt forward and seized his arm, sinking brown teeth into his wrist. Forcing his left arm to work by sheer will, Slocum drew his left-hand Colt and shot the man through the neck.

It was all going bad. Slocum could sense it. The men

from Calvary should have broken and run at the charge. They hadn't. Now the line of horsemen was spread out, each man isolated in the midst of enemies who sooner or later would overwhelm them. Slocum saw young Charlie McBride dragged off his handsome buckskin. Strong as a bull, the boy managed to wrest himself free of his captors and race toward his friend Doug, who was lashing out with his coiled lariat in a frantic effort to win through the mob. Then a burly man with a mat of black hair hanging over wild blue eyes stepped forward and slammed a pickax into the boy's stomach. A bullet instantly brought the man down, but as Charlie staggered, bloodied hands clutching the implement embedded in his body, he was struck simultaneously by an ax and a hoe, and then another man buried a pickax in the meat of his shoulder. *"No!"* Doug Travis screamed as his friend fell and was lost to view under flailing tools.

"Slocum! Behind you!" At the sound of Velarde's voice Slocum spun in the saddle and pumped the last three rounds in his Henry through the body of a man stooped over to slash at the paint's hamstrings with a small sickle. Velarde was laying about him with the Winchester. Then he swayed in the saddle, and Slocum saw a red spot appear on the Mexican's white shirt, just above his left hip.

"Santiago! Run for it!" Slocum shouted. He laid the barrel of the Henry across the nose of a man grabbing at his reins. Lafe Carrihew rode across Slocum's field of vision, fleeing, with a bloody and battered White Eyes clinging to him from behind. Velarde's pain-filled eyes met Slocum's. The Mexican wheeled his bay mare and raced away, back toward the herd.

Slocum followed, emptying his pistols, hacking left and right with the Henry, with no thought now but to get free of the savage horde, the weapons that smashed and stabbed, the hands that clawed until the owners fell in death. Something hit him in the small of the back. His vision blackened and the breath left his body. *This is it*, he thought. But the paint gathered himself and with a mighty leap sailed free of the mob. Clutching the saddle horn with a white-knuckled hand, Slocum managed to keep his seat and his life.

The others had gotten free ahead of him—those who were going to. Santiago, swaying drunkenly in his saddle, Lafe and White Eyes, Shag Coltrane with his left arm limp, the sleeve soaked in blood, Doug Travis, whose eyes streamed tears as he cast a last look back at the place where his friend had fallen. Though a score or more of their own lay dead, the men of Calvary were running in mad pursuit, still singing their song at the tops of their lungs.

Cookie was still kneeling near the wagon, which had rolled to a stop, methodically reloading and firing into the onrushing mob. "Get the wagon turned around and get out of here!" Slocum yelled.

"The Lord *is* my shepherd; I shall not want . . ." With a shock John Slocum recognized the words the mob had been singing as it fought. Over and over they were chanting the Twenty-third Psalm.

He came even with the wagon as Cookie got the mules moving, drawing the vehicle in an agonizingly slow arc. His Sharps pistol boomed defiantly at the enemy as the wagon turned around.

"Yea, though I walk through the valley of the shadow of death, I shall fear no evil: for thou *art* with me," sang the citizens of Calvary, Kansas, as under the approving eye of their prophet they began methodically to slaughter the foremost steers of the drove.

"Thy rod and thy staff, they shall comfort me."

14

As the first hint of pink began to tinge the band of cloud lying on the eastern horizon, John Slocum finished muffling the nose of his horse with a flannel shirt and turned to peer out a crack between two boards of the warehouse wall. The street outside was still deserted. But it wouldn't remain so much longer. He'd found this hidey-hole not a moment too soon.

The steers had not been so lethargic that they would stand by for long while they were killed with mauls and picks. The mob had killed a dozen or so, and the rest had turned and gone fleeing back the way they'd come, streaming in a bawling line past the hill where the vultures and the crows squabbled over the fruits of the three strange trees. Only prompt action by Cookie had saved the new chuck wagon from meeting the fate of the old.

With the Jebusites decisively on the run, the men of Calvary had been content to turn around and go trooping back to town, singing psalms, bearing their dead and injured with them. At their head rode Reverend Coffin, as grave and silent as a statue.

It was past midnight before the uncontrolled flight of the steers was checked. Slocum had been compelled to order Velarde to dismount and lie down in the wagon under Cookie's care; the Mexican was determined to help halt the stampede though he was bleeding freely from his bullet wound and could barely stay in his saddle. Coltrane permitted Carrihew to bandage his badly hacked arm, and then he got back on his horse to chase the stampeding animals. The others were all in condition to carry on, once White Eyes got a new mount from the remuda. A pitchfork in the chest had brought his own down beneath him, and Lafe Carrihew had barely reached him in time to save him from the fate that had overtaken young Charlie McBride.

When at last the steers were halted, several miles from the now dark and silent town of Calvary, Slocum had returned to the wagon to see how Velarde was doing. Cookie met him some distance away. "It ain't good," the big man said in a voice pitched low so as not to carry. "Ball's still in him, and I been afraid to probe for it. Didn't hit him square in the gut, so he's got a chance. But . . ." The huge, sloping shoulders shrugged.

Slocum nodded. It felt as if the skin on his face were dried like parchment, tightening on the bones. A man shot straight through the belly died, always, no question—sometimes long and lingering and raving with fever, sometimes in minutes or hours. But always. Velarde might have a chance.

It wasn't likely to be a good one.

"How's it going?" Slocum asked as he climbed into the wagon. He had an oppressive sense of always coming into this canvas sepulcher to tend the shattered hulks of those he cared for.

The Mexican managed a gray smile. "I tell you the truth, señor, I been better," he said in that bantering greaser accent he affected when he was being sarcastic.

"Yeah." Slocum held up a bottle of whiskey. "Want to drink?"

Velarde shook his head. "Don' know where it would

come out, *ése*." A wave of pain crossed his face and he shut his eyes.

"You'll have to leave me," he said.

"Do you think we can find a way past Calvary?"

Velarde smiled without opening his eyes. "You'll think of a way. Just find some friendly family and leave me with them. I'll get by."

John Slocum reached out and briefly gripped Velarde's hand. Then he left the wagon. Within minutes he was riding through the dark toward Calvary.

The street was beginning to fill up with people. Men and women in pairs and groups walked by the warehouse. Slocum could hear no slight chatter, no conversation. It seemed that the townsfolk went about their morning business in the same eerie silence with which the men had awaited the charge of the riders yesterday.

Everybody seemed to be moving in one direction, along a wide street that, though no more than a dusty strip, showed sign of being frequently dragged with heavy logs to keep the surface even. They were going to church, he realized. It was Sunday. He'd forgotten the fact.

He'd told his comrades that he was hoping to pull off some sort of trick or diversion upon the townspeople, that would occupy their attention while the J-Bar-C steers ran past. He had no idea what he could do, only that such a scheme was their only hope—unless they wanted to wait till the rivers subside, which wouldn't happen any too soon, to judge by the black clouds hanging off in the north, their insides occasionally shot through with lightning.

But Slocum had another reason for sneaking into Calvary. He was determined to seek out Chastity Coffin and confront her. She seemed a different order of being from her fellow townspeople, the grim fanatical men, the women now walking by with faces dour beneath plain bonnets, and especially different from her merciless, thunderous father. He tried to justify his quest by hoping she might intercede for him and his men if he got a chance to speak to her. Deep down he knew his desire to meet with her again sprang from sources far more fundamental.

He bided his time, hunkered over among the crates, watching the citizens make their unspeaking, purposeful way toward the church in the center of town. He marvelled again at the neatness of the settlement. The raised sidewalks were swept scrupulously clean, the buildings shone with fresh coatings of whitewash. The pitched roofs of town weren't missing a single shingle that Slocum could see. Even in this hail country, each window had its scrubbed and shiny pane of glass. Even storehouses had spotless exteriors.

That was what had worried Slocum when he'd led his horse into the town in the grey of the false dawn. Every prairie town he'd been in, no matter how small or newly sprung from the sod, had its share of disused and neglected structures. He sometimes had the impression the settlers put up shacks first, and then erected structures such as dwellings, stores, churches and town halls.

Calvary was the exception. Because they were labelled in neatly painted signs he found several storehouses, but all bore signs of frequent use. He needed a hideout, a place to leave his horse, and it wouldn't do to leave the animal where any local was liable to wander in for a keg of nails. He was just beginning to despair of finding anyplace in this unnaturally well-maintained town that he might have a chance to hide, when he glanced in the window of this lonely square structure a couple of streets from the town square. Inside in the dim half-light he saw piled crates and what looked like bolts of cloth.

Leading his horse by the reins, he walked around to the broad side door for a closer look. Like every other building he'd seen this one lacked any lock. The door opened to a push. He stepped inside and lit a match, carefully masking the flame from the window with one hand.

The first thing he saw was that the contents of the room were cloaked in a layer of the pervasive, invasive red dust of Kansas. Everywhere else in the town that he had seen, the inhabitants had found some magic way to ward off the ever-present dust, even in the other storehouses he'd examined. Frowning at the mystery, he investigated closer.

Only to find a deeper mystery. The bolts of cloth, brightly colored, some splashed with bold, gay patterns. The sort of stuff to tickle feminine fancy—but not that of women whose menfolk lived and died to the call of a living prophet, and sang psalms while they massacred strangers. He looked over the crates. *Liquor*. Mostly whiskey, some brandy and other such truck. And there was a box of band instruments, tarnished cornets and flutes and snare-drums, carefully packed away. And here was a box of popular novels, and a stack of brittle copies of *Ned Buntline's Yellow Journal*.

It was a storehouse filled with all those fripperies and luxuries which a stern folk like the Reverend Hezekiah Coffin's flock would delight in denying to themselves.

He'd led the paint inside and shut the door. He tied the horse where it couldn't be seen from the window, and sat himself down beside a slight crack, judging it safer to watch through. He waited.

He'd given up puzzling over the problem of the warehouse's curious contents long before the last longfaced citizens, hurrying now lest they miss the service to which a bell in the steeple imperiously summoned them, had vanished from the prim street. Instead he had begun again to think of Chastity. A rising fever of excitement and impatience gripped him.

So intent was he on his thoughts that he didn't hear the muffled snort of his horse that indicated someone coming near. Nor did he hear the soft turning of the door on its hinges, well-oiled like all of Calvary's hinges. Nor the quiet step behind him.

"Howdy, stranger."

His heart was in his throat as he whirled, gun in hand. A man stood there silhouetted against the still-weak morning light. Unfazed by sight of Slocum's cocked Colt bearing on his midriff he shut the door softly behind him. "Looks like it's going to be a fine day, don't it?"

Squinting, Slocum studied the man. He was the first shabby article Slocum had seen in Calvary: a small man, stooped, one shoulder hiked well above the other in a marked hump. He wore a ratty coat and baggy trousers with holes in the knees, and the soles of his shoes flopped beneath. A strong odor of stale whiskey wafted from him, and even in the murk Slocum could tell his face had only occasional commerce with a razor.

"The name's Simon," the stranger said affably. "Do you like what you see, friend? You're eyeing me as if I were a yearling colt you were thinking of buying."

"I'm lookin' for one good reason I shouldn't drop you where you stand. Amost did. What the hell you come pussyfootin' in here like that for?"

"One good reason for not shooting me is that my esteemed fellow citizens would come swarming out of their place of worship like angry bees from a hive, intent on working mayhem on you. I believe you've had a sample of their malice already?" Slocum could not keep down a wince. "Yes. You're one of the individuals from the cattle drive that tried to pass the town yesterday. Well, friend, you've seen the little welcoming sign the burghers erected. If you shoot me you can expect about the same." He uttered a driftwood laugh. "Not that they love me so much. They simply hate strangers more."

Ignoring Slocum's gun, he walked by, pried up a loose slat on a crate, and fished out a bottle of whiskey. "Ah. At least I'm well provided with the staff of life."

Beginning to feel a little foolish, but unwilling to give up his advantage, Slocum lowered the pistol. "What in God's name do they keep this stuff around for? Figgered they'd want to burn it."

Simon laughed again. "Perhaps for the same reason they keep me around. As a reminder of what they're giving up. The Reverend Coffin, God bless him—and He will, unless He is a total ingrate—is fond of pointing to me as the end product of leading a life of sin. 'Behold this twisted creature, this wretched scum of the earth, and look on the very wages of sin!' Of course, I was born with the hunchback, and had to achieve the rest of my present estate by dint of diligent effort. But we must allow our resident messiah a measure of poetic license, mustn't we."

Slocum sat down on a stack of cloth-bolts, raising a cloud of dust. He let in the hammer of his Colt and slid it back in its holster. The bent little man obviously meant him no harm. If he had, all he'd needed to do was slip off to the church without ever making himself known to Slocum, and return with the Calvaryites with their hammers and railroad spikes.

"What in the name of hell is going on in this town?" he demanded.

Simon threw his head back and laughed. "Nothing, in the name of hell. What the people of Calvary do is all in heaven's name."

"Shut up, you danged fool!" Slocum hissed.

Simon doffed his hat, poked fingers mournfully through a hole in the crown, then brushed at his balding pate and greasy brown hair with a grimy hand. "They are sitting in the pews, immersed in the thunder of the Reverend Coffin's latest sermon. If you shot me, they'd have heard. But nothing less noisy than a gunshot has a chance to be noticed." He put the hat back on. "What's going on here, you ask? They call it the Lord's work. Another might call it insanity. Cotton Mather would be no stranger to it. Nor Torquemada. But I perceive those names hold no meaning for you."

"What do you know about a girl named Chastity?" He blurted out the words before he knew what he was doing.

A light glimmered at the back of Simon's glass-bead eyes. "Ah, you've seen her? You love her then." Slocum blinked at his bald assertion. "Don't be surprised. For a man to lay eyes on the Reverend Coffin's golden-haired daughter is to love her—to be consumed by love for her." He dropped his whiskey tenor voice an octave. "And lust. Yes, that too."

"You mean all these religious Johnnies too?" Slocum's tone was frankly skeptical. "I'd think their heads'd be too full of thoughts of the Holy Ghost or whatever."

"Oh, they are. But the men of this town, each and every one, lusts after Chastity Coffin. Being filled with the Spirit doesn't deaden a man's appetites, my nameless friend, at least not the brand the Reverend dispenses. What has happened in this town is that its denizens have thrown reason out the window, and sworn to live entirely by their passions—which the good Reverend Coffin keeps whipped to a fine lather. And Chastity too, in her way. For she is that which no man can resist, the virgin and the whore, innocence and depravity, a bitch-goddess with the eyes of a child." Slocum couldn't follow the funny little man's fancy talk, but somehow he understood what Simon was driving at. Deep down in the gut he understood.

"And she knows it," the hunchback said. "She flaunts herself, teases the poor rubes every chance she gets. Are you familiar with the ancient and honorable sport of bear-baiting? No? No matter. That's what Chastity Coffin does. Though I think the original pastime was kinder."

"But I saw her down to Hudson, in a buckboard driven by one of those wild-eyed boys of the Rev's. Lantern-jawed feller, young, with big whiskers and funny dead gray eyes."

"That would be young Nehemiah Scudder." Simon nodded. "Some say he desires Chastity Coffin more than any other." He shook his head. "I might contest that, but no mind, no mind."

"But how the hell can the Reverend trust his daughter with a crazy man like that, out alone on the prairie?"

"Because much as Nehemiah lusts after Chastity, he fears hell more. And if any spark of intellect still simmers somewhere in the recesses of his Neanderthal skull, he fears her father even more."

"I have to see her," Slocum said.

The little twisted man laughed until tears rolled down his cheeks, eroding the dirt caked on his pinched features. Slocum glanced nervously around. Simon had a laugh much too big for his diminutive frame, and Slocum wasn't convinced the sound of it might not attract attention.

"You got to take me to her. I have to talk." He licked his lips. "It's, ah, about my drove. I want to ask her to talk to her daddy about letting us past."

"Indeed." Simon dabbed his eyes with a befouled handkerchief. "Well, my mysterious stranger, what can I do but lead you to her." He gave Slocum an appraising eye. "There aren't many like you in this town. Perhaps she might, ah, listen favorably to your request."

With Simon scuttling in the lead, they stole from the warehouse. The little hunchback displayed a surprising swiftness and agility, and longer-legged Slocum found himself hard pressed to keep up with him as they moved cautiously from building to building. Simon was as masterful as any scout Slocum had known in making use of cover, darting from alleyway to rain barrel, dashing across a side street to hunker in the lee of a parked wagon.

By a roundabout route they came to the town square. It was as immaculate as the rest of the town, though it was no more than a square patch of clay, flattened by scores of tramping feet, around which neat frame buildings stood like nuns. Slocum and his guide peeked cautiously around the edge of the barbershop. "There's the church," Simon said, pointing at the unadorned building with its wooden steeple. A covered walkway connected it to a two-storied building with a prominent veranda. "That used to be our city hall," the hunchback explained. "Reverend Coffin took it over when he assumed the functions of temporal government as well as spiritual. He lives there." He moistened his lips. "Chastity too."

"She there now?"

Simon shook his head. "She sits in the foremost pew,

and watches her father orate with adoring eyes."

"So we have to wait—"

Slocum never finished the sentence. From behind came a shout of "Hey! Who's that there!" Slocum spun to see a party of men approaching with their lethal implements over their shoulders, led by a young man riding bareback on a plow horse with a rolling-block rifle in his hands.

"Dear God, they sent out patrols overnight!" Simon exclaimed. He grabbed Slocum's sleeve and ran for an open alleyway.

A shot crashed as Slocum dove into the alley on Simon's heels. A moment later Slocum heard a commotion from the church as the faithful began to pour out to investigate. "It's one of the Gentiles," he heard a young voice cry. "He has the reprobate Simon with him!"

The two of them pelted headlong through the alley as the crowd took up the chase, baying like hounds. They dodged through the spotless streets and finally sheltered in another alley. The sounds of pursuit drew inexorably closer, and Slocum knew that soon he would have no place to hide.

Simon looked up at him. "I may be a true Calvaryite after all," he said, "a natural slave to superstition. But I feel you were sent here for a purpose." His eyes flickered toward the street, from which came shouting and the drum of running feet. They were on this block and coming closer. "God help me if I'm wrong. In fact, God help me period."

He gripped Slocum's arm with surprising strength. "Circle around and come upon the town hall from behind. And give no thought for me, or what I do is in vain."

"What are you talkin' about?"

For answer the little man turned and ran out into the middle of the street.

"There he is!" a voice blared. The other manhounds gave tongue. Simon turned as if surprised, gaped at the onrushing mob, then dashed away up the street, out of Slocum's view.

John Slocum ducked into a doorway until the crowd streamed past the mouth of the alley. Then he turned and ran for all he was worth.

Totally spent, John Slocum leaned against the rear of the town hall and gasped for breath. Sprinting from cover to cover, senses as fine-tuned and alert as a wild animal's, he had followed Simon's final instructions and made it to his destination unseen, while the enraged townsfolk hunted the hunchback. The effort had wrung him out like a bar rag. He was a hard man and fit, but it had been a long time since he'd had anything properly describable as rest. He was nearing the end of his tether. *Just hold on a little longer,* he told himself. He thought of Chastity, so near now, and his heart beat a little quicker.

He edged around the corner of the building. There was a side entrance here. He moved toward it carefully and then stopped.

A crowd had gathered on the red clay square. They were silent, so silent he hadn't known they were there until he saw them, though they weren't forty yards from him. A wagon, laden with something extremely heavy from the way it rode low on its strings, had been drawn up by the square. Whatever was in the bed was covered by a tarp. The Reverend Coffin stood on the driver's box and faced the crowd. As Slocum watched, he raised his arms. "Bring forward the accused," he intoned.

The crowd parted and Simon was thrust forward. He went to his knees before the preacher and stayed there swaying as if too weak or stunned to rise. A bruise mottled half his face, and trickles of dust-caked blood ran from his nose.

"You." Coffin fixed him with a pointed finger. "You were seen consorting with an accursed Gentile. How do you plead."

Simon rocked back and forth. "He forced me," he moaned. "He was sent to spy out the town, and made me guide him to the church. Please, your reverence. He held a gun on me. I had no choice."

"Where has the son of Baal gone?"

"Why, I think he must be trying to return to his comrades." The little man wiped half-dried blood from his nose. "If you hurry, you might be able to catch him."

"Liar!"

Simon fell face forward before the preacher. "Mercy! Have mercy on me! I did no wrong!"

"Men of Calvary!" The Reverend raised his arms above his head. "For too long have we sheltered this viper at our bosom. Now he repays our kindness by consorting with blasphemers. And what is that?"

"Blasphemy!" howled the mob.

"And he that blasphemeth the name of the Lord, what surely shall befall him?"

"He shall be stoned!" It was a shriek of blood lust. The crowd surged forward to the wagon and tore back the canvas covering. The wagon was laden with rocks, ranging from fist-sized to the size of a man's head. Eager hands caught up the stones.

"No!" Simon leapt to his feet. He ran. He ran fast for such a bandy-legged little man. But not fast enough.

A rock glanced off his shoulder. He staggered.

Another hit him in the kidney, and Slocum clearly heard him grunt with pain. A shower of smaller stones enveloped him, flung by the women, who cawed at him like carrion birds. He dropped to his knees again, holding up both arms to shelter his head. Then he battled to his feet and once more trotted forward, across the square. The crowd followed, clutching armloads of stones.

A burly man took up a huge stone two-handed and heaved. It took Simon between the shoulder blades. He pitched headlong. With excruciating effort he raised himself from the dirt and raised himself to a sitting position, facing the mob that stalked him.

"Hear me, Calvary!" he screamed. "Your hours are numbered! The instrument of God's wrath is at hand. *Mene, mene, tekel upharsin*—thou art weighed in the balances, and art found wanting—"

A hamhock-sized stone struck his forehead with a crunch. His eyes glazed. Slocum saw the curious depression in the dome of Simon's skull, and then the hunchback fell onto his side thrashing like a dog run over by a stagecoach. The mob closed in, stones held high, to smash, to crush.

His teeth grinding together in fury, Slocum ghosted up the steps and into the town hall.

He found her on the second floor, the third door from the landing, at the front of the town hall. Like every door in Calvary, it was unlocked. He turned the knob silently, pushed it open, and there she was.

Her boudoir was a plain room. There was a window, covered with blue-trimmed white curtains against the ugly scene taking place on the square below, a bed with a blue-and-white spread and plump feather pillows, a white painted dresser before which she sat combing her golden hair in an oval-framed mirror. She wore a white nightgown trimmed in blue, long-sleeved and chastely high-necked.

She turned to look at him as he stepped inside and softly shut the door. Infinite calm showed in her sky-blue eyes. "I was expecting you," she said.

He blinked. "You was?"

She rose and set the brush down. "When I heard of the brave man who dared to defy my father yesterday, I knew it must be you. The strong, handsome man I saw in Hudson."

He fought down the rising lump in his throat. "I—I come here to talk to you."

She smiled. "I know what you came here for." She walked forward. He tried not to watch the sway of her heavy round breasts beneath the cotton gown, but their motion was hypnotic, irresistible.

She stopped an arm's length in front of him. He raised his eyes to hers. What he saw there made his knees turn to water.

She raised slim white hands to her throat, pulled at the blue ribbon tied around the slender column of her neck. As if by magic the gown fell away from her body. Slocum's breath caught in his throat. She was far more beautiful than he had imagined—glorious, naked, her skin the color of fresh milk, her breasts exquisite in form, the nipples the palest pink and taut with eagerness. Her waist was slim, her belly rounded and firm. The fur between her gorgeous thighs was spun gold. A single dewlike drop glittered in the strands of hair curled across the pale pink lips of her sex.

"You desire me." Her high, musical voice dropped. "What do you wait for, stranger?"

Involuntarily Slocum's eyes flicked toward the door. She laughed. It was a sound like silver bells. "No one will disturb us." She grasped his wrist in cool fingers and tugged him toward the bed.

He came along docilely, putty in her dainty hands. She stopped beside the bed and her fingers began to work nimbly on the buttons of his shirt. When she had peeled that garment from his unresisting body she sat on the edge of the bed and unbuttoned his trousers. He came alive enough to help her, pulling the pants down his muscular legs, kicking off his boots and stepping out of the trousers. She let her eyes slide up his body, and he felt his already rigid manhood stiffen further.

"Beautiful man," she said, "what's your name?" Her eyes were a cat's eyes, predatory, demanding.

"John Slocum," he husked.

"Well, John Slocum," she said, lying back and parting her perfect thighs, "take me."

He leaned forward, took his weight on his arms and lowered himself atop her. His fatigue sloughed off like a snake's old skin. His arms quivered as he descended, but not from weariness.

She sighed as the tip of his penis touched her. With a spasmodic motion of her hips she drove herself onto him, and her arms dragged him down onto the beckoning softness of her breasts.

Her body moved with a suppleness and strength that made him gasp. She rolled herself around him, caressing the length of him with cunning tightenings until sweat ran into his eyes and he moaned aloud. Too soon, he felt himself explode within her. His fists closed around wads of bedclothes as he drove himself into her with all his strength.

She cried out and raked his back with her nails like a she-panther. When he was spent she locked her luscious legs about him and rolled over, so that she straddled him like an alabaster colossus, her breasts looming over his face. "I'm not finished with you yet, John Slocum," she whispered. Her hands raised her breasts, proferred them, and she leaned forward as her hips began to roll and roll about him.

How many times she drew him on, brought him shuddering and groaning to climax as outside the day wore on to afternoon, he never knew. He only knew that she gave him the most intense pleasure he had ever experienced. Even his lovemaking with Ellie, his dark flame in the night, paled to insignificance.

He thought of Ellie once as they lay side by side with his hips sliding slowly back and forth, Chastity with her eyes half closed as she urged him on with sweet, urgent words. Thought of her, but could not recall her face. *Ellie*, he thought. *Ellie, forgive me.* Then the powerful muscles of Chastity's belly were contracting as she cried out shrilly in her own pleasure and her nails dug into his arm, and thinking went away.

She offered him a deep pit and a narrow well, and her lips dripped with honey and her mouth was smoother than oil. That angel-innocent girl, not even twenty, taught him things he'd never known or even suspected. And always she demanded more of him, and always, or so it seemed, he found that he possessed an inner reserve of strength to match his unending hunger for her.

At last they quenched the fires of their passion and lay entwined in each other in a sweet state between sleep and waking. She teased his ear with her small pink tongue, then carefully traced his jawline to his mouth and kissed him. Then she rose and donned her gown. He watched with a certain smugness as the chaste folds of cloth covered the splendid half-globes of her rump. Then his eyelids slumped and he let himself drift toward sleep.

Chastity padded to the door and opened it. Two men

stood there, broad-shouldered men with mad eyes and faces hard as granite. One of them was young Nehemiah Scudder.

Slocum's eyes snapped open. His mind, fuddled by weariness and repletion, couldn't grasp what was going on.

Until a slim white finger pointed at him. "There's the Gentile," Chastity said. "Take him."

15

He tried to fight them. They brought out truncheons and clubbed him senseless. He knew nothing for a time but red throbbing pain, and blackness.

Suddenly he was drowning. He sputtered and shook his head and broke the surface of the water. Then his eyes opened.

"That's brought him around, Reverend." Nehemiah Scudder stood back, holding a bucket in his blocky hands.

He was on his knees on the mirror-polished hardwood floor of a sparsely furnished room. Late afternoon light slanted golden through narrow windows, warming the wood so that it gave off an odor of varnish, and a lingering hint of long-ago tobacco smoke that not all the scrubbing of the Calvaryites could banish. Iron manacles held his wrists.

In front of him to either side stood Nehemiah Scudder and another young man who might have been a twin, or at least a near cousin. Beyond them was a large walnut desk. Neat piles of paper occupied the wide top, and an immense black-bound book lay open in the middle. Behind the desk stood the Reverend Hezekiah Coffin, peering down on Slocum over the tops of half-moon glasses.

"You are a foolish young man," the Reverend said. His voice was oddly quiet. Perhaps he kept his trumpets in reserve for pulpit and battlefield. "You should not have come."

Slocum glowered at him. His head pounded with the slow beat of a military frog march. He was acutely aware of his nakedness, and of the horrible danger he was in. But he was determined to show no weakness.

"I have to get my drove to Abilene," he said.

The Reverend Coffin sighed. He walked to the window with the weighty tread of a man bearing a great burden and looked out over the square at the town he ruled. "It is an awesome thing to hold the destiny of several score souls in your two hands. To provide temporal guidance as well as spiritual for an entire town. Especially in this wicked, godless age."

He turned from the window. "You've caused me a great deal of trouble, Mr. Slocum. You have deprived this town of many hands needed to do the Lord's work. And your interference today compelled us to take the life of one of my own, a man whose soul I had determined to save in spite of the best efforts of himself and Satan." He help up a hand, palm upward, fingers outstretched. "Simon's salvation was within my reach, Mr. Slocum. His blood is on your head. Likewise his damnation."

"How about the hands of them that killed him," Slocum snarled. He tried to rise. Young Scudder grabbed him by the hair and dragged him back down to his knees.

"Tools of God's justice, Mr. Slocum. Even as my poor self."

"You butchered two of my men and hurt another so bad he ain't likely to live," Slocum said, voice rising in fury. "Is that your God's justice? If so I say to hell with it, and with you, too!"

Scudder cuffed him to the floor. His ears rang, but he continued to glare at the Reverend.

Coffin shook his head sadly. "You tried to bring pollution to Calvary."

"All's we tried to do was run our cattle by."

"Your diseased kine. But that's not all. Your men would have wanted to come into town. They would have tried to corrupt my people with their godless ways. The spiritual health of this community is a fragile thing. It has only recently been lifted from sin. I have hopes . . ." He raised his eyes to the ceiling. "I have hopes that one day Calvary will become a modern City of God, burn as a beacon for the whole Christian world to follow to true salvation. Such is my mission. Such is my dream. Surely you can see I could not permit you to spoil it."

He walked back behind the desk. "My people are pure, but they are not yet grown mature in the knowledge of Christ. They must have their faith buttressed from time to time. And there is no surer way to strengthen their faith than by displaying the swiftness and sureness of God's retribution. The unfortunate Mr. Lancer—a friend of yours, I believe—and his associates provided me with an excellent opportunity to vindicate the might of God. Now God has sent you to me, to reinforce the lesson. Therefore your fate shall be suitably instructive."

Painfully Slocum hauled himself to a sitting position. "Spit it out," he said raggedly.

"Very well. Lift him up, boys." The two burly Calvaryites grabbed him by the elbows and drew him up onto his feet. "Do you see that stake the workmen are erecting in the square?" Slocum nodded. "One hour after sunset this very evening you will be bound to that stake and burned until you are dead, Mr. Slocum." Coffin looked at him with a thin sad smile. "Please believe me when I say I regret the necessity of such harsh measures. But it should console you that your death will do much to further God's great plan."

A glob of Slocum's spittle struck him under the right eye. He recoiled, his black eyes blazing with outrage.

Slocum felt a fist slam into his kidneys like a pile driver. He doubled, gagging and cursing, and the two men dragged him from the Reverend Coffin's office and down the hall. There was a door there with the first lock John Slocum had seen in Calvary. They opened it and threw him in headlong. He lay groaning on his belly as the door slammed at his back. He heard a key turn, a tumbler fall with the finality of a headsman's ax.

He raised his head and looked around. It was dark in here but for a few stray shafts of light penetrating the boards nailed over the windows. The room was perhaps nine feet square and utterly bare. The Reverend took no chances that the subjects of his moral lessons might speed themselves on their way and cheat his wards of their spiritual instruction.

The sun was almost down. In two hours, maybe less, they would be coming for him. *Burning alive*. The thought made his skin crawl.

He sat up, held his head in his hands. Nothing seemed broken, although it felt swollen to twice its normal size. Quickly he checked himself over.

He didn't seem to have taken any permanent damage from his treatment so far. That was good. To carry out the plan beginning to form in his mind he would need every bit of strength, skill, and cunning he possessed. And more than a touch of sheer hell-burning savagery.

His lips peeled back from his teeth in a smile. That last should be no trouble to summon up. No trouble at all.

"All right, Gentile, on your feet," said the fat man as he pushed open the door. "We got to get you ready. Can't have you goin' out in public buck nekkid. Frighten the womenfolk something awful."

John Slocum lay in the far corner of the room, coiled about himself in a tight knot of pain. He rolled half onto his back, moaned, and hugged his belly tighter and rolled back to face the wall.

One of the sturdy young men who accompanied the swag-bellied turnkey looked reproachfully at the other. "Satan gnaw your vitals, Nehemiah. You done busted his gut when you hit him."

"I din't either, Hosea. I know how to hit better than that."

A tongue like a pink sausage flicked over the fat man's lips. "You boys better do something fast," he said in a curiously high-pitched voice. "He dies now, Preacher'll have the three of us take his place."

"Perdition!" Nehemiah spat. "I tell you I din't hit him that hard." He walked over to Slocum. "Get up, you." He kicked the prostrate figure.

Slocum screamed, a broken sound that ended in a gargle. "Lord of mercy, Nehemiah," Hosea exclaimed. "You kilt him."

"Naw." But Nehemiah's face had gone pale beneath his bristling whiskers. He bent down and gripped Slocum's trembling shoulder. "Gentile. Gentile, speak to me. Are you ill?"

John Slocum opened his eyes and looked at him. "I'm just fine, pigfucker," he said.

Nehemiah's jaw dropped. Like a striking rattler Slocum uncoiled, pushing off from the wall with his legs, swinging the chain with the full force of both arms. The heavy links caved in the young man's left cheekbone and carried away his nose and upper lip. For a moment Slocum stared into two gray eyes staring hideously over a death's-head mask of red blood, white bone, and grinning teeth. Then Nehemiah shrieked and fell to the floor.

Hosea had a navy Colt revolver halfway out of his

belt when Slocum leapt at him and caught him in the temple with the chain. His skull popped like an eggshell and he fell, blood and brains drooling onto the floor.

The fat man tried to run. Like a cat Slocum was on him, whipping the chain around his neck and driving a knee into his flabby back. The turnkey tried to scream as the links bit into his pasty flesh. His eyes rolled like the eyes of a frightened steer, and his tongue jutted from his mouth, already going purple. His saliva showered Slocum's face, and his hands beat ineffectually at his attacker.

With a grunt of effort Slocum broke the man's windpipe and lowered him to the floor. The man rolled from side to side, clutching at his ruined throat while his face blackened. Finally his struggles ceased. Slocum knelt quickly by his side. He had a gunbelt buckled around his vast belly, with a Remington in a cracked leather holster. Slocum pulled the belt off him and fastened it around his own waist, though even at the last hole it drooped around his hips. Next Slocum relieved Hosea of his navy .36. He left the prison room, carefully shutting the door and locking the three corpses inside. The key he slid under the door.

Hosea's pistol in hand, Slocum padded down the hall. It was nigh onto full dark outside. A single kerosene lamp burned at the far end of the corridor, past the door to the Reverend's office. Its yellow light barely reached this far.

At the door to the preacher's office Slocum stopped. To his amazement he heard a voice inside. It was the Reverend himself, and he seemed to be practicing a sermon. *Can't hardly believe it*, Slocum thought. *Didn't he hear that infernal ruction?*

As quietly as he could, Slocum cocked the navy. Then he put hand to the doorknob, turned it oh so carefully, and opened the door a crack.

The Reverend Hezekiah Coffin was there, all right, standing before his desk. He wasn't alone. His black trousers were puddled down around his ankles. Kneeling on the glossy floor before him was his daughter Chastity, still in her white-and-blue nightgown. Her mouth was open, but her eyes were shut in ecstasy. The Reverend had both big hands rested lightly on his daughter's golden head, as if administering his blessing. His hips were rocking gently to and fro, and he was murmuring, "For Thine is the power and the glory forever and ever Amen . . ."

For a moment Slocum stood there too stunned to move. Then he gathered himself to spring into the room and interrupt the tender family scene. Both father and loving daughter—what hostages they'd make!

"I wonder what's keeping them," he heard a voice say. "They should have brought the prisoner out five minutes ago."

John Slocum leapt back from the door. Footsteps were coming down the stairs at the far end of the corridor. "Fat old Zebedee's probably snuck off to raid the larder," a second voice said.

The first one chuckled. "More likely Nehemiah's got a head start chastising the Gentile. It's the sin of gluttony, I say. He's already claimed the right to light the bonfire."

By this time Slocum was into the room across from Coffin's office, shutting the door softly. He was in a disused records room, filled with filing cabinets. He listened at the door as the voices passed. "Sheol!" one said a moment later. "The door's still locked."

"You were right, brother," the other voice said. "It was Zebedee's belly that got the better of them, not Nehemiah's wrath."

Slocum heard Coffin's door opening. "What's going on here?" the Reverend demanded. A bit breathlessly, Slocum thought.

"Zebedee and the others haven't collected the prisoner yet."

"Those sons of Belial! If they delay the prisoner's expiation, I'll have the hide scourged off their backs!" Slocum heard the door close again, and three sets of footsteps dwindling down the hall.

When they were gone, Slocum emerged. He crossed rapidly to the other door, flung it open, leapt inside. Chastity sat on the edge of her father's desk, a dreamy look in her pale blue eyes. It changed rapidly to alarm as she saw Slocum. "How did you get here?"

"I walked through the walls," Slocum gritted. "On your feet, missy."

"What are you going to do?" She held a hand protectively up before her breasts. The contrast to her attitude of a few hours before caused him to give a maniacal yelp of laughter.

"Lot less'n you deserve, if you do like I say. Otherwise I'll give you a taste of your daddy's medicine—and not the kind he was givin' you a moment ago. Come on!" He gestured peremptorily with the muzzle of the gun.

Hesitantly she came to him. He thrust her roughly into the hall and began prodding her along the corridor to the door he'd first entered by, away from the church. She kept looking fearfully over her shoulder at him, chewing on her full red underlip with her faultless teeth.

They were almost to the door when a man came down the stairs and turned the corner to face them. "My God!" he exclaimed.

"Give him my regards," Slocum replied, and shot him through the chest.

Shouts came from above, the sound of booted feet

stumbling down stairs. Slocum leaned around the corner and fired twice. He heard a wail of pain or fear. Spinning, he grabbed Chastity by the wrist and hauled her off down the corridor in the opposite direction as a gun barked in the stairwell.

A hallway met the long corridor like a short upright of a T, leading from the front entrance. Men were piling in through the front door as Slocum and Chastity crossed the mouth of the passage. He squeezed off his last two shots in passing and tossed the gun away.

"You can't hope to get away with it," Chastity gasped as they reached the door at the far end of the corridor, which opened into the covered walkway to the church.

Slocum yanked open the door. "You better hope I do, bitch," he said. "Move!"

She pulled away from him as they entered the church proper. They had come out near the altar, in the shadow of the raised pulpit. As Chastity turned to race up the nave to the double doors, bare feet slipping on the floor, John Slocum drew the Remington, took careful aim, and fired.

Splinters exploded from the top of the foremost pew. Chastity shrieked and clapped her hands over her ears. She stopped running.

"I wouldn't mind blowing off one of your pretty little legs and dragging you along with me," Slocum said. "Wouldn't mind it at all."

The front door burst open. Slocum shot the first man through the door. An unknown number of companions yelled in alarm and fell back.

On the other side of the altar from the pulpit was a door. Slocum guessed it led up to the steeple. He seized Chastity's arm and pulled her to the door.

Booted feet thudded in the covered walkway. An angry tumult grew outside the double front doors of the church. There was nowhere to go but up. Slocum opened the door. "After you, mam'selle."

With an angry glare Chastity stepped past him and mounted the ladder. She climbed three steps and stopped. "No. I won't go."

He jammed the muzzle of the Remington in between the cloth-clad cheeks of her rump. "You'll climb," he growled, "or I'll shove this in to the cylinder."

She climbed.

He followed, judiciously prodding her buttocks with the pistol to keep her serious-minded about things. She pushed the trap open and hoisted herself up onto the platform with the bell rope, affording Slocum a look at her legs and higher reaches that under other circumstances would have interested him greatly.

He pulled himself up after her, keeping a wary eye on her. She slumped against the sloping wall and showed no further sign of resistance.

Voices came from below. Slocum snapped the trapdoor open and fired into the most astonished expression he'd ever beheld on a human face. The body of the enterprising climber fell back on his companions.

"I got lots of powder, caps, and shot," Slocum hollered down. "Just keep sendin' the boys up."

He heard the scuffle of retreating feet and congratulated himself on his tactics. Until he heard the distant cry, "Bring torches! We'll burn the sinner out!"

"But he's in the church!" another voice protested. *Lissen to him,* Slocum mentally urged the townspeople.

The stentorian voice of the Reverend Coffin rose above the din. "He has defiled our place of worship. Let it therefore be his pyre. See how futile it is to flee the Lord's wrath, John Slocum?"

In truth Slocum was beginning to feel hopeless. He thought he'd escaped the flame, but all he'd really won was a bigger pile of kindling. And somebody to face the flames with him, he abruptly recalled.

Each face of the steeple had a window at the level of the bell platform. Slocum flung open the one at the front and stuck his head out. A sizable crowd had gathered in front of the church, and several score torches were raised against the night. "Coffin!" Slocum yelled.

"I'm here, sinner. Have you decided to give yourself up and face God's vengeance like a man?"

"No. Have you decided you want to barbecue your own loving daughter?"

A gasp rose from the crowd. "He's lying!" a woman exclaimed.

Slocum turned from the window, reached down, and wound his hand in yellow hair. He dragged Chastity to her feet and held her at the window for all to see. "Here she is. If I burn, she burns too."

The mob spilled around the side of the church, trying to get as close as possible. "Stand back," Slocum warned them. He touched the barrel of the Remington to the frozen-faced girl's temple.

Alone, head bowed, the Reverend Hezekiah Coffin stalked along the street that ran down the side of the church. He stopped beneath the steeple and looked up. His black eyes caught and held Slocum's gaze.

"As Lot was willing to sacrifice his daughters which had not known man, so that the men of Sodom would turn from his door," he intoned in his rich, deep voice, "even as Abraham was prepared to sacrifice Isaac, his best-loved son. So must I, in the name of God." He turned to his followers. "Let it be done."

"Daddy, *no!*" Chastity screamed. Coffin turned away.

Below his feet John Slocum heard the sound of breaking glass, and the *whoosh!* of spilled kerosene taking fire. He smelled smoke at once, heard a roaring as fire began to eat at the wooden pews beneath.

His mind raced, trying to take stock of the situation. He had the easiest shot in the world at Reverend Coffin's broad back. But much as he hated to admit it, killing Coffin was a last resort. If he did that, he'd never leave Calvary alive.

His nose wrinkled at the first acrid taint of smoke in the air. The mob was beginning to press in at the side of the building, braving the heat that built within, faces upturned, eager. Eager to see the flesh of the outsider blacken and crisp at the searing touch of the fire.

A thought tickled the back of his mind. An idea, but he couldn't grasp it. *Think. Think hard, damn you!*

Slumped at his feet, Chastity put her small fist to her mouth and coughed. Then she gave a cry of alarm. "The floor! It's getting hot!"

Gazing out the window, he nodded. He could feel it in the soles of his feet.

She threw herself at him, wrapped her arms around his knees. "Don't let it happen," she moaned. Tears coursed down her cheeks. "I don't want to burn. Oh, Johnny, I didn't mean it, my father made me betray you."

He didn't deign to dignify that by pointing out its obvious absurdity. She stroked his thighs imploringly. "Oh, Johnny. Take me away and I'll love you forever. Get me out of here. They won't hurt you if I'm with you. Oh, John, I'll make you happy. You know how I can make you happy!" She kissed the head of his flaccid penis.

When that didn't move him, her lips slid forward to enfold him. He started to push her away, and a voice spoke in the back of his mind. It wasn't the voice that usually spoke to him, that inner Slocum who was scathing and skeptical of all things the outer one did. It was the voice of Simon the hunchback.

Think back to your Sunday-school lessons, my

mysterious friend, the voice said. *You heard what the man said about Lot's daughters and Sodom. He's just given you the keys to walk out of here.*

Slocum bit his lip. It was hard enough to concentrate without the preacher's daughter doing what she was doing. *Remember what I told you about the men of this town—and Chastity Coffin?*

"*Yes!*" John Slocum shouted to the skies.

Chastity quit and pulled her head back to look at him. He smiled down at her, bent down, and helped her to her feet. "Oh, John, I knew you wouldn't let me burn," she said, smothering him with kisses.

"Wouldn't dream of it," he said, and ripped the nightgown from her.

Her blue eyes went wide with shock. He pulled her to the window. "John, what are you doing?" she shrieked.

Wordlessly he pushed her out, keeping a tight grip on her arm. The crowd below grew very still.

The naked girl huddled against the steeple, her toes gripping the shingles of the pitched roof, her frightened animal's eyes staring down at the upturned faces. "Here she is, boys," Slocum called down. He stuck the pistol in the holster and grabbed Chastity by both shoulders, turning her so that she was exposed to the crowd in all her glory. "This is what she's been wagging under your noses for so long. How about it."

An animal growl rose from the mob. "Blasphemer!" Coffin screeched. "You dare not! You'll insure yourself the flames of hell."

"Better'n the flames lickin' at my backside now, Rev," Slocum said, and threw Chastity Coffin down to the waiting crowd.

She shrieked. A score of hands caught her, lowered her gently to the ground. And held her there as the pious men of Calvary began to tear off their clothes and crowd around.

Chastity kicked and struggled, wailing like a lost soul. The Calvaryites crowded round, laughing and jostling, battling to get to the naked lithe form. "No!" roared the Reverend Hezekiah Coffin. "Get back, you animals! Let my daughter go!"

For the first time in any man's memory, the men of Calvary flat ignored the commands of their preacher.

With a high-pitched cry of despair the Reverend flung himself into the crowd, beating at them with his great fists. Then a naked man as broad as a barn door turned and stretched him out in the dust with a single blow of his fist.

John Slocum was scrabbling crab-fashion along the roof of the church toward the front. It felt as if his ass and the soles of his feet were frying. He paid the discomfort no mind. In a moment he was away from the mob, which had converged on Chastity now. He slid down to the gutter, leapt to the ground, and ran like hell for the storeroom where he'd secreted his horse.

Thanks, compadre, he thought, feeling foolish.

His imagination—it must have been—answered, *Thank you, my nameless friend. You made me a better prophet than old Coffin.*

Then he was at the warehouse. His paint gave him a reproachful look as he tore open the door. He jumped on the animal's back and rode like the wind.

And so it was that John Slocum, naked as the day he was born and still in chains, led the J-Bar-C drove past the flaming pyre that men had called the town of Calvary.

16

The tearsheet calendar hanging on the wall behind the counter of the railway freight office said Tuesday, September 6, 1870, when Slocum walked in out of the morning sunshine and asked the clerk, "Where's the Frenchman?"

The clerk laid the jack of hearts on the queen of spades and glanced up at Slocum from under his green eyeshade. "Who?" He started to move a pile of cards topped by the ten of clubs to put it on the jack.

The pile of cards flurried to the floor as Slocum grabbed him by the lapels and hauled him up onto his feet. "The French colonel, LeBlanc. *Where is he?*"

Unruffled, the clerk extricated himself from Slocum's grip. "Gone." He glanced down peevishly at the cards strewn about his feet.

"Say what?"

"Are you deaf? I said he's gone."

Slocum felt the floor start to open up beneath him. "But—" He could say no more.

The clerk looked at him sidelong. "Oh. You came here after that bonus he was offerin' for steers on the hoof." He shook his head. "Sorry. Too late."

"Did some other outfit get here first?" Slocum asked desperately.

"Oh, no. Colonel pulled up stakes and left three days ago. Got some kind of telegram."

Slocum stood there with his jaw hanging open, unable to believe it. Jimmie Fitzhugh, Ray Polder, Dane Andersen, Lonesome Dave, Charlie McBride—even Blaylock and Bogen: the men who'd died to get the herd through. In vain. Ellie and Santiago Velarde—the woman he'd loved; the friend who'd saved his life, hurt bad and maybe dying. Joe Callahan, waiting impatiently in his wheelchair back in Mora County, waiting for word of how his big gamble had paid off, not suspecting the fate of his daughter.

All for nothing. *Nothing*.

The stricken look on his face penetrated the clerk's irritation. "Here, this came through yesterday on the train from St. Lou," he said, reaching under the counter. "I reckon the colonel's departure had something to do with this." He laid a thick newspaper down in front of Slocum.

With blurred vision Slocum leaned forward and read. It was a copy of the New York *Herald*, dated September 3. PRUSSIANS VICTORIOUS IN FRANCE, a headline screamed. Beneath it: EMPEROR, FRENCH ARMY SURRENDER; FRENCH KNOCKED OUT OF WAR IN CRUSHING DEFEAT AT SEDAN, AUGUST 29.

Without a word John Slocum turned and walked from the office. There wasn't anything left to say.

With a clatter the Wells Fargo stage pulled away from the Abilene station, carrying with it the proceeds of the J-Bar-C drive in a locked strongbox, under a heavy guard. For the sale of the fourteen hundred seventy-six head of steers that survived to reach Abilene, at thirty-five dollars a head—premium prices, as the purchasing agent said, just before Slocum knocked him down—the

J-Bar-C received $51,660. According to the arrangement he'd made with Slocum at the outset, Joe Callahan was to receive three-fifths of that, or $30,996. As trail boss, John Slocum was to receive $10,332, and the survivors were to split a like amount.

It was a goodly sum of money. Slocum's share was more than he'd ever had at one time, or maybe earned in his whole life. But it wasn't a drop in the bucket compared to the quarter of a million dollars the herd had been worth when it left the J-Bar-C. Slocum had resolved to alter the arrangements a bit on his own initiative, though he hadn't yet told anyone.

All the J-Bar-C crew except Slocum were riding back with the Wells Fargo stage. As Slocum stood on the boardwalk breathing in the dust raised by the coach horses he saw Cookie's bearlike arm waving from the cabin of the stage, and one by one the riders waved to Slocum as they rode by, Lafe Carrihew, Shag Coltrane with his arm in a sling, White Eyes looking happy at the prospect of getting back to his squaws. There was a stinging in Slocum's eyes as the cavalcade pulled away down the street and was lost to sight.

He heard the noise he'd been waiting for, a boot on the wooden sidewalk behind him. Doug Travis was standing in the doorway of the Wells Fargo office, hands at his gunbelt. Slocum looked at him calmly and said nothing.

"Mr. Slocum," the boy said tentatively. "I swore to kill you when we reached Abilene."

"That's right."

The towheaded kid blinked down at the ground, then raised his eyes and faced John Slocum square. "I was going to say that there's been enough killing already. That's true, but it'd be the coward's way out to say it. So I'll tell the whole truth. I was wrong to say I'd kill you, Mr. Slocum. Everything you done, you done the best you know how, and I don't know nobody who coulda done more. It was a damnfool thing to say, and I take it back." He swallowed. "If you want to kill me, Mr. Slocum, it may just be you got the right."

Slocum gazed at him until the blue eyes lifted to meet his. "Ain't it time you started calling me John, for God's sake?"

Doug blinked, then grinned. "Sure thing—John." He stuck out his hand. Slocum shook it.

"You got your money?"

Doug nodded. "And Charlie's, too. I—I guess it'll be some comfort to his maw and his sisters." None of the other dead men—Polder, Lonesome Dave, even young Jimmie Fitzhugh, whose folks had been killed by the Chiricahua—had family. So it was agreed to split the money among the survivors, but with a full share set aside for Charlie McBride's people. There was less money to go around than anybody had expected, but there was still a lot, and none of the men who'd been through the hell of the drive together felt much like being tightfisted with his comrades.

"I gotta go, John," Doug said, unhitching his horse from the bar and swinging into the saddle. "You take care of yourself. I hope . . . I hope I get to ride with you again someday."

"Thanks." He watched the boy ride off in pursuit of the Wells Fargo wagon and his comrades. He hadn't been able to make himself say he hoped so too.

He wouldn't wish such a fate on any man as to ride with John Slocum.

He walked over to his paint and rubbed the animal's nose affectionately. His saddlebags bulged with provisions and money. There was Santiago's share, and Ellie's share. And John Slocum's share, as he had privately reckoned it: $1,135. A hundred and thirty five of it was for a month and a half's work at the standard ninety bucks a month a trail boss got; the thousand dollars was a bonus, since, by God, Slocum had been through a hell of a lot more hell than any normal trail boss.

But more than that he couldn't accept. John Slocum was not a man who failed to respect money, and the promise of the Frenchman's gold had drawn him onward through unimaginable hardship. But he hadn't won Joe Callahan's big gamble for him, and so he couldn't make himself take his full share of the reward.

He mounted the little paint. The animal tossed its head, as if a night in the finest stable in town had made it eager for the open spaces again. If he rode hard, Slocum might reach the sodbuster's hut where they'd had to leave Santiago sometime tomorrow afternoon. And though he wasn't a religious man—especially after the catechism he'd received from the Reverend Hezekiah Coffin—he said a silent prayer that the Mexican would be able someday to enjoy his money in good health.

And then Slocum was bound for Hudson and Ellie. He didn't know how he'd look her in the eye, much less how he could face her father. But he would.

"C'mon, you scrubby little sonofabitch," he said to his paint. "Let's ride." He touched spurs to the horse's flanks and galloped off into the eye of the setting sun.

JAKE LOGAN

NERO WOLFE

BLACK ORCHIDS
BY REX STOUT

THE GRAND MASTER OF DETECTION

The World of
Rex Stout

Now, for the first time ever, enjoy a peek into the life of Nero Wolfe's creator, Rex Stout, courtesy of the Stout Estate. Pulled from Rex Stout's own archives, here is rarely seen, never-before-published memorabilia. Each title in the Rex Stout Library will offer an exclusive look into the life of the man who gave Nero Wolfe life.

Black Orchids

The first Bantam cover of *Black Orchids*, from 1982.